YOUTH AT RISK

YOUTH AT RISK

TRICIA YOST

Radial Books

Also by Tricia Yost
First Things
Votives: Entries from the Daybooks of Gertrude Tate, 1898-1952
Factory
All That Is Behind Us Now

Published by Radial Books
radialbooks.com

Youth at Risk / Tricia Yost, 1st ed.

ISBN: 978-0-9984146-4-5

Cover Art: *Lost Opportunities*, Anette Lusher, 2011.

Typesetting services by BOOKOW.COM

We all have reasons
for moving.
I move
to keep things whole.

MARK STRAND, "Keeping Things Whole"

Though they dabble, girls who wind up at Harrington Gardens aren't cutters, anorexics, or pill poppers. Internalizers end up locked in hospital units or in dedicated, private rehab facilities. Harrington girls externalize. They rage. They destroy homes and cars and public property. They rip chunks of dyed threads from expensively styled heads. They throw bricks through windows and steal whatever they can. Yes, they might drink and smoke and fuck and cut. They might self-starve, swallowing their emotions like heroin balloons, but that's not what gets them to The Garden.

Vic stole smokes from the corner store and threw lit ones at her three-year-old half-sister in a city park, igniting a fire.

C.H. ran over-the-counter pills and tubes and supplies from drug stores to cookers in the country.

Carmen stole prescriptions and stamps and jewelry from old folks at the home where she volunteered. She stole cats from neighborhoods and sold them to dog fighters.

Lydel gave head to truckers for money and drugs until she sliced the thigh of a guy who'd smacked her around.

Anna, arrested at a house party, was holding a rainbow bag of pot, speed, cocaine, and unidentified pills. Too large a cornucopia for personal use. Days before, she'd been thrown out of a movie theater for shooting a pellet gun at the screen.

Nesha, surprisingly sober, was found guilty of simple assault and disorderly conduct.

Kyle. Name it. She did it.

Misdemeanors, near felonies, the least of what they've done, the least of who they are.

As most of you know, The Garden sits on forty acres of forest and trails with several clearings for individual and group activities. Wooden plank bridges cover boggy deposits of leaves and sticks and moss. A mixture of density and openness. A quarter mile to the west of the building we're in, a large clearing looks toward water, that huge plate of salty sea. At the far edge of the clearing, an unused donated telescope rusts in the weather. Past that, into the woods is a partial adobe hut, a project, long unfinished, of a former resident. In an attempt to be sustainable, one of the staff pushed for a community garden. The girls—the residents—have outdoor chores such as weeding, planting, and trail maintenance. Beyond all the cultivation stands a tall stone fence topped with coils of barbed wire. Our own Great Wall, our own separation from Mexico. The girls can run for miles, in circles, zigzags, but ultimately the facility holds them. Sequestered thirty-five miles to the northwest of Portland, this squat compound holds bunks and classrooms, a cafeteria, a gymnasium, and physical and mental health offices. If any of the girls got to the roof, she wouldn't fall far. Even if she were stupid enough to dive headfirst, she wouldn't guarantee herself a broken neck or swift end.

Skinny-throated Kyle, who always held her head in a contracted tilt of suspicion, jumped twice, earning bruises and sprains, a dislocated elbow, and a broken fibula. When she arrived at The Garden, she didn't say more than ten words for two weeks. She didn't smile for three. Laid out in the infirmary on day four, she sweated and shook. She barely registered my existence when I introduced myself as the resident psychologist, offering my availability if she wanted to talk. Prior to entering The Garden, she'd subsisted on weed, acid, E, speed, and the occasional line of coke. To stay hydrated she drank cheap, watery beer. Two weeks prior to her bust for crashing a stolen car into a postal box, she'd tried meth and tried it again. And again after that. And then she tried heroin.

"I'm not crazy."

"No one said you were."

"Fuck off then."

Wracked by withdrawal and tremens, her own body a stranger assaulting her, Kyle hadn't cared who I was or who she was. She wanted the torment to stop, but could do nothing but vomit and sweat and shake and spit and shit, and repeat these actions for days. When her body finally wrung itself out, she went to a room in residents' hall. There, in the bunk, her body quiet, her mind started screaming. Then she started screaming. She was no different from the others. Everywhere the same.

"You got a boy's name, bitch."

"Fuck you."

First group, first sober words.

I liked her immediately.

Nearly every hour scheduled, the girls move between group therapy, school classes, work duty, breakfast, lunch, dinner, individual sessions. No idle minds, no idle hands. The six components of The Garden: *Story*. Of course. Tell and retell. Story is the foundation of everything. *Transparency*: explain everything. Be direct so everyone, staff and resident, knows what's expected of them, and when, where, and why. This ensures energy is not wasted worrying or struggling over unknowns. *Focus*: give appropriate attention so the residents know key figures are interested in their thoughts, emotions, activities. Implicit in this is to focus on their strengths. Build the girls up; don't break them down. *Choice*: limited, but available. Possibility is paramount. The residents need to feel a sense of control. They need to enact their will in safe, structured environments. *Challenge*: complex opportunities for change. Goals. Achievement. Challenge amplifies positive resilience. Challenge circles back to strength, further reinforcing what the girls are good at, their successes. *Imagination*: the roof or sky, the air. Reinventing themselves. Reimagining their stories, their lives. Full circle.

The six pillars, my idea, got me this job. Having finished the didactic portion of my PhD in Clinical Psychology with a dual specialization in criminal and adolescent rehabilitation, I'd completed a year internship at the Junction Center in west Detroit, a secure confinement facility that housed fifty-two male offenders ages twelve to seventeen. After that trying year, I didn't want to work with boys in their blind rages in a facility whose only purpose is containment. The Garden, one of the few private not-for-profit facilities, which had opened its doors a mere eighteen months prior to my interview, was still finding itself, still open to fresh ideas. Edna Harrington, whom I hear will sit in on these proceedings tomorrow, the wife of Graham Bernard Harrington, III, Oregon judge, spawned Harrington Gardens after her husband was killed by a twenty-two-year-old female he'd sentenced when she was twelve. Edna, a spry seventy-four, sat in on my interview. After nine minutes of conversation, she stood to leave. "Hire her," she said. I felt chosen and full of myself. After that, I only saw Edna at holiday parties and occasional fundraisers. She'd put her team in place and disappeared.

After her first jump from the roof during week three of her program, Kyle lay unmoving in the infirmary. "I'm beginning to think you like this part of the facility," I said, dragging a chair closer to the bed.

"Don't get comfy."

"I wouldn't like it. No one to talk to."

"You can't take a hint?"

"The sooner you start talking, the easier things get."

We sat in silence, me looking at her, her looking at everything but me. The clock's second hand chugged its infinite circles.

"I have all day," I said, legs crossed, hands resting peaceably on my knee. My back resting against the chair's plastic hold.

Finally Kyle said, "Talking's overrated."

"Why's that?"

"You hear the shit they say in here?"

"All day every day."

"Whole lotta nothing."

"I disagree."

"You have to."

"You'd be surprised what talking can do for you."

"Yeah? Can it stop my leg from throbbing? Can it stop me from wanting to shove my fingers into some girl's eyeball?"

"You'd be surprised."

"This is how it fucking goes? I tell you shit and you talk like that shriveled dick, Yoda? A year and a half of *this* before they let me go?"

"Is that all the time we have together?"

"You're not funny."

One by one, I lay out the stones. Different shapes, different textures. The girls can pick them up, roll them through their hands, consider them, consciously or subconsciously, each one perhaps a brick toward a rebuilt psyche.

"You're not helping yourself with these stunts," I said.

"Who cares?"

"I do. We all do."

"You're paid to care."

"True, but I also choose to be here." I tugged at a thread in my shirt cuff. "Why did you jump from the roof?"

"Because I could."

"You climbed up there with a broken leg. That took some effort."

"So what."

"That shows me you can do anything you set your mind to."

"Whatever."

"You have resolve. I'd prefer you use that sort of energy for other things aside from self-destruction," I said.

Kyle, arms tight across her chest, clenched and unclenched her jaw.

I waited, part strategy, part aggravated inertia.

"Vacation," she said. "There are too many things to do all the fucking time in this place."

The success of this program, as you've heard, depends on unwavering structure, on safety and dependability, which were not regular components of the girls' experiences. Safety and dependability are, however, foundations of the facility's mission.

"Why can't they give me something stronger than Tylenol?" she asked.

"You know why."

"It's bullshit."

"What's bullshit?"

"You dumb or something?"

"I'm asking for clarification."

"Fuck your clarification. My fucking leg hurts. My elbow hurts. I don't want my leg or elbow to hurt."

"I don't think that's what hurts."

"You're the one who should be locked up."

"Your jumping and wanting pain meds, there's a bigger reason for those behaviors than wanting to skip class or group."

Quiet again. Again the insistent clock. Its fixed radius.

"Tell me something," I said. "Tell me a story. That's where we start. With the stories we tell ourselves. Be specific. Everything's in the details."

"Dude, you're flat-ass batty."

Kyle did start talking. Eventually they all start talking. Everyone wants to talk. To be seen. Heard. Understood. Everyone wants out of themselves at any cost. Sometimes you have to ask questions to get the process started. Sometimes the process has already started.

"I'm number four. My mother never married. She doesn't know for sure who the father of the first two are," Kyle said. "My dad's been in jail since I was three. I sent him letters, you know, when I learned to write. All my third grade year. We were supposed to be writing some shit pen-pal in England and I was writing my dad in prison. I still don't know what for. I would tell him stupid stuff. Subjects I liked. Gym class. I was always picked first of the girls."

"You were athletic?"

She shrugged.

"You were tough?"

She smirked.

"What subjects did you like?"

"I liked writing. I liked concentrating on each letter and then the whole word. For the longest time I did the 'e' backwards. And geography. I liked that. Whole damn huge world out there. Kinda blew my mind. The teacher, wack job like you, told us about places in the southwest that had energy fields that helped people. Isn't that a weird thing to teach third-graders? This thing that was out there was so mysterious. I told my dad about it, thinking maybe he could go there. But the fucker never wrote back. I suppose you're gonna ask how that made me feel—like he's a fucker. That's how I feel."

"Angry?"

"Whatever."

"I'd be angry if I put myself out there, wanting to connect with my dad, and then didn't get anything in return."

"I'm not you."

"That's not about you, Kyle. His not writing back. You deserve his letters and attention. He, for whatever reason, couldn't give that to you. But that's not about you. You know that, right?"

"The fuck you say? He doesn't give a shit about me. How is that *not* about me?"

"That's his selfishness, his loss."

"Do you have enough for a diagnosis now?" she asked.

The girls clutch their defenses. They keep trying to resist, trying to protect themselves.

"I'm not so fond of diagnoses."

"Some doctor you are."

"A diagnosis is a collection of symptoms. It's not a cause or reason. It's a dead end like a label or stereotype. Not useful, and often harmful and limiting. Lives, events, are so much bigger than any diagnosis can handle. Nothing is ever so simple."

"You're saying you can't handle me?"

"I'm saying the labels can't."

"We know why *we're* here. Why the hell are you?"

They all ask this question. I ask it myself. I saw early that there were no new strides to be made in the private, secular treatment of the modern adult. In America, our sicknesses vary on a theme: affluent malaise. Solidified, no matter what Maud had tried to tell me, back then under her tutelage. Maud Greggor, an analyst I worked with for five years from the end of undergrad through my PhD, always seated in the corner, her tiny frame with its dowager's hump hidden beneath a large cloak, and her pale, arthritic hands resting naked and accusingly in her lap. That relic tried to convince me the psyche was infinite and there would always be more to learn about treating it. Tried to tell me that everyone needs help toward self-knowledge and actualization. "Core work," she'd said. I hated those words. Together they sounded pithy, inaccurate, as if analysis were a Pilates session. I'm conflating therapy and analysis, I know, but you get the point. I didn't think rich people didn't have problems. They did, just not ones as real as those of the non-rich. Someone like Kyle, for example. Real work gets done with the Kyles of the world. In the inner city, in prisons, shelters, juvenile centers, in group with me.

"I'm here because adults are boring," I told Kyle. "Teens live in a heightened state of emotional chaos and development. I can make more of an impact with teens than with adults. Plus, I was a teen once. I was lost at your age and wished there was someone around to guide me a little more than my parents could."

"Fuck kind of psycho-shit is that, dude?"

I laughed. "Please don't call me dude."

"What's funny?"

"Psycho-shit. That's funny."

"No one else has to do four days a week. Am I your biggest project? Don't people spend years and years talking in circles?"

"Some."

"That's some shit, isn't it?"

"You have years and years. You have a whole life ahead of you."

"Not of this, I don't."

"You don't have to live how you've been living. Your life is yours. Make it what you want."

"You keep saying stuff like that. I don't buy it. And why should I? My whole life has been weird dudes hanging around my mom and sisters and no food and teachers kicking me out of class and police staring me down for standing around."

"Your whole life? There was a time you were hopeful. There was a time you were curious about things, like geography and your dad."

"See where that got me?"

"It's still in there, that hope, that curiosity."

"Nah. Long gone."

"I think you know there's something else out there for you, a different kind of life. I bet there isn't a day goes by that you don't think about it."

"It ain't worth it. People out there," she pointed toward a wall, waving her hand beyond it, "they talk and talk and never get anywhere."

"You're afraid that you'll feel like you do now for the rest of your life. You won't. You think you will, but you won't. You'll see things differently. You'll feel things differently."

With her father in prison, her mother drugging in an abandoned building, and her siblings dispersed in foster care, I decided, after weeks of seemingly idle conversation, to have Kyle sit in on family sessions. Having her do so might spark other memories. Having her do so might get her out of her own head sooner. Might help her realize she's not so alone.

Lydel, slumping as far as sitting in a chair would allow, kept her pale arms crossed tightly into her chest. She clad herself in black: T-shirt, jeans, mascara, shoes, nail polish. Her hair, already dark, she'd dyed darker just two days prior. I had trouble picturing the woman Lydel might become when she grew out of the bitterness and into some color.

"What else could I have done? I have to work. I have to pay the mortgage. I can't be home all the time," said Gloria, Lydel's mother, who was seated to Lydel's right. Gloria wore two-inch heels and two-inch bangs, fuchsia lipstick, and an uncomfortably tight-looking skirt. Her ankles bulged over the edge of her shoes. I tried to gauge if her trashy power-suit, her appeal to basic male instincts, was working for her. From Lydel, I'd gleaned that, notwithstanding a series of short-lived boyfriends, Gloria had been a single mom forever. That day her fourth digit sported only wrinkled skin and a mall tan.

"Lydel," I said, almost as an exhale, "do you have some thoughts on what you would have liked or would now like from your mother?" Stock-speak. I was trying to cruise through the day. I pinched at my own ring finger. Alice and I hadn't bothered with rings or a ceremony, both feeling we didn't require the attention, nor want the gifts and obligatory pleasantries of a reception. While we never hid our fondness for each other, we didn't advertise it either. At two years in, our verbal commitment to each other had been enough, and four months ago we etched five years together.

Lydel stuck a finger up her nose and drew down a dry green mass and flicked it. "That's my thought," she said.

Since early that morning before the parents arrived, Kyle had not looked at me once. She didn't want to participate in family session, and, as it always did by mid-morning, an internal restlessness took hold of her, which that day had manifested as petty orneriness. At breakfast she'd picked at and complained about the food. She whined about the water pressure in the showers. "Lydel," Kyle said, "that's fucking gross. Give us something real for once."

"Bitch, you starting with me already?"

The two held an unspoken, agreed-upon animosity toward one another.

"Forget it," Kyle said. Her gaze moved from shoe to shoe to shoe of the people in the group: a brown loafer of some sort, scuffed at an odd spot on the insides of the big toes; heels, Vans, Chuck Taylors or their cheap knock-offs; a pair of men's work boots, crossed at the ankles. Road construction by the looks of the dust all over them. The boots belonged to Carmen's father, a squat man with a permanent pained, confused expression. The type of man who believes if you work hard and keep working hard things will turn out well. The fact of his daughter, only fourteen, in a stay at The Garden, deepened the creases in his face. I could hear the tape looping in his head, "I don't get it. I just don't get it."

Sitting next to Carmen's father: Pete, Anna's stepfather. Kyle kept shifting away from him. The chairs were too close, and Pete's thick, tanned forearm with its shiny watch expanded onto Kyle's armrest so that in order not to be touching him she had to tuck her elbows in, drawing further away and into herself. She couldn't bear to touch him, even innocuously. Worse, he was oblivious to the space he occupied.

"I know how you feel, Gloria," Pete said, causing Kyle to inch farther right. "There just never seems to be any getting through. We hit a similar wall with Anna. Just at wits' end, having done everything we could. Psychiatrists. Anti-depressants. Tough love. Nothing helped. Or things would help for a week or two, but then she'd get right back into the things she was into."

An ass was what he was. He looked at Gloria in a charged way, flirting with her. Using his problems with his kid to get a sympathy fuck. Where was his wife today? Not that Anna wanted to see her, but The Garden requests that both parents, if not irreconcilably estranged, show up on family day. This was the third Thursday she'd missed.

"We tried everything, but we just couldn't compete."

Most of the girls' parents are children themselves. From the very start I couldn't stomach Pete and continually struggled to find anything at all likeable about him. He was a big man who knew it and used his size to intimidate. And when he wasn't trying to intimidate, he pandered and played the role of the good father. "Pete," I said, obligated, "try to be as specific as possible. What are the 'things she was into' that affected you?"

"The drugs. Lying. Stealing. She didn't think we knew she was stealing, but we did."

There he was again telling Anna what was and wasn't in her mind. She knew they knew she was taking things. She didn't care. She was testing them, seeing how much she could pilfer before they'd finally take action. Her experiment started with change from Pete's Washington Monument Tower jar. Next a bracelet from her mother's second bureau. Then the DVD player from the lower level of the house, which she pawned for cash she didn't need. She had a generous, unearned allowance. Pete and his wife made plenty of money. Anna kept going, item by item, removing bigger, more noticeable objects from the house. Only when she took a limited Francis Bacon print did her mother say "Are you curating your own museum now?

The Anna Munro Family Museum? I want my Bacon print back, Anna. You have no right to take my mementos." To which Anna, stoned, uncaring, said, "Sorry. Fenced. Gone. Good thing, too, it wasn't much to look at." This was a lie. Anna liked the print of a reclining figure, presumably female and naked, on a fainting couch or operating table, in obvious anguish and quite vulnerable. She told me the print made her think of violence and isolation. Her head hurt to think she shared this liking with her mother and that her mother had any aesthetic sense. Because Anna was so angry and annoyed to have something like this in common with her mother, she carefully took down the print, removed it from the frame, and meticulously rolled it into a protective tube. She then hid it in the back of her closet and hung the empty frame back on the wall.

"Anna? Would you like to comment on what Pete just said?"

"No." She had been listless and hadn't said much for several days, which worried me. I walked the thin line of pursue-retreat. When pushed or questioned, she retreated. She had to come to me.

Pete didn't bother shifting his weight toward the girl he'd been raising since she was two. "You've got to have *something* to say for yourself." Entering his fifties and bulking in the middle, Pete was an ex-marine. While free of the Corps' physical reigns, he had never dropped its self-righteousness and superior attitude. He regarded himself as if he remained in top mental and physical form, still agile and capable of anything. Yet Anna's behavior called his capability into question, and though he could not admit it to himself, he felt threatened, small, weak, and altogether embarrassed to be sitting among such people, unable to control this teenager. "Maybe you'll have something to say about this. Your little friend, that tweaker who stole my boots, came by last week."

Pete was talking about Egan, a boy Anna had seen on and off over the last year. Egan, a sophomore who covered the bathroom mirrors in the school with black spray paint, had been making his second pass and was in the girls' bathroom drawing sexual scenarios on toilet seats and stall doors with silver paint when he opened the door upon Anna, seated sideways with her feet on the wood of the opposite wall. The two ditched school for the rest of the day and rode Egan's scooter to Marine Drive to kick around in the Columbia and watch planes take off and land. According to Anna the two were nearly inseparable after that. She went with Egan to all the parties they could find. She liked getting high and drunk or taking speed and making out with him. When he dyed his hair jet-black, she dyed hers orange. When she pierced her navel, he pierced his left nipple. Anna's parents weren't pleased with her "little acts of rebellion," but Egan, though he dressed in faded, cut-off army fatigues and never combed his hair, was genuinely polite. He'd help set the dinner table and clear away dishes. He recommended to Mrs. Munro that she stop wearing so much brown and try shades of blue because they went better with her skin and eyes. Anna didn't care if her parents liked Egan. He thrilled her. He was fun, and though he wanted sex a lot, he didn't push for it like Anna's other boyfriends had. He was content to spend afternoons lying on the banks of the Washougal, staring at a cloud-enveloped sun. Egan also always had weed, which Anna liked smoking. She liked the airy feeling that swooshed through her head and the indolence that coursed through her limbs. Pot made her feel everything was okay. Egan had different reasons for smoking. He claimed pot unleashed his subconscious and put him in touch with the muses. "Two of them," he'd told her. "There are nine, but I only need two." Anna didn't wholly buy his reasons. When pot landed them both in trouble, however, nobody cared about either of their justifications.

"I knew it was you," Anna said. She clamped her lips tight and looked at the ceiling, fighting back tears.

I've seen every kind of parent-child visit. Awkward, stuttering ones, tearful, heartrending ones, steely, silent ones, and loud, knockdown ones.

Pete shrugged. "He came by. He wanted to take a picture of that shit in the garage. His *grand mural.*"

Egan and Anna constructed a space for themselves in the empty, damp attic of her parent's garage. They nailed sheets of plywood to the rafters and beams and covered those with inches of blankets. They lit candles and kept lots of flashlights ablaze. Egan had dry-walled the slanted ceilings and painted. He'd slashed out violent, fiery strokes of red and brown. With a jug of wine at his feet, he'd spend hours working the makeshift canvas, painting and repainting while Anna watched. He claimed to be painting a mural of his mind, depicting how enraged and out of control he felt. And, as if to enact this, sometimes in the rain he would strip off his clothes and run howling through the neighborhood late at night. Anna didn't believe he was tortured. He was only playing the tortured artist. He wanted to be great and thought doing drugs and running wild was a way to travel to the imaginative side of the universe and bring genius back with him. Of course she loved him.

"And?"

"And what? He's a weird little twit."

"You're a prick."

"Don't talk to me that way."

"Fuck you. I will always talk to you this way. I hate you. You're a liar. You cheat. You're an asshole. You do whatever the hell you want, when you want, with no regard for anyone."

"You're a little bitch, growing into a fine bitch. You're in for a hard life. You know what I did when he showed up? I led him out to the garage, made him climb the stairs, and take a good look around. His masterpiece? I ripped that thing apart. I threw away your love nest and painted the walls. Coated them with buckets of white paint. Buckets and buckets," he sneered. "Took me hours, but it looked like any old freshly-painted attic."

Anna stared darkly at the man she would never call her father. "You're the asshole that pushed him over the edge. If you think I'll have anything to do with you ever again, you're wrong, fucking wrong." Anna bolted from the room, knocking her chair to the floor.

Later in the day, when I found her alone in one of the classrooms, she showed me a square piece of cardboard with an ink drawing on it. A deep, red, snakelike river twisted in convolutions on the card. Behind the river, under it, two naked figures, a male and female, formed a circle with their bodies. She'd gotten the drawing in the mail the same day Egan's mother called her. Egan had hung a belt from a beam in the basement, helmeted his head in a plastic bag, and beat off, going for the ultimate orgasm. Months before Anna was sent off, Egan had talked about trying it. She was terrified he'd kill himself in the process and had dissuaded him with countless blowjobs while choking him a little with her small hands. In her dreams after he died, she saw his face frozen behind clear plastic, his eyes fixed and wide, his lips curled in agonized pleasure.

"I don't fucking want these bitches or their parents knowing anything about me," Kyle said. She hated family group. We were alone for an individual session. "You should be thankful I'm even talking to you. Makes your job so much easier, doesn't it?"

"I am thankful. I enjoy talking to you."

"Why do you have to say shit like that?"

"It's a compliment, Kyle. I think you're deflecting. I don't think you mind if others know things about you. That's not what this is really about."

"Oh, tell me, Guru, what is it *really* about?"

"You're the only one in group without a parent."

"With parents like that, who wants parents?"

"They show up."

"Whatever."

That day, Kyle, still fuming, couldn't be seduced into meaningful conversation, but she was beginning to trust me. And talk. She became someone who couldn't not talk. At her age, I was the opposite, keeping everything in, watching the world evolve around me, rarely participating. I marveled at the talkers.

"It ain't shit, Shrink. I think you know that. Deep down beneath all that psycho-shit and story-babble, you know, nothing can be done. No one can be helped out of themselves."

"That's not true," I said. I had to disagree. Claiming otherwise would render void the last decade of my life. Some days, though, I questioned my value, what difference, if any, I was making. I had to continually convince myself that saving the youth of America was the last best cause.

"I've got no one."

"You've got me."

"You don't count."

"That hurts my feelings."

"I don't have *family*."

"You've got siblings."

"Two are cracked-out and I don't know where the other one is. You know why I did meth the first time? I was trying to bond with my sister. I got a little rock, a quarter-gram. She was so excited, thinking it was her birthday. She taught me how to fire it up and smoke it. All they say about that white nugget is true. I felt fucking fantastic for hours."

"You can feel that way without drugs."

"Not *that* way."

Then Kyle told me this:

"My sister wanted to do it again. We went to this guy's house who she knew. It was totally sketchy, but with my mom missing for days, dad in jail, I didn't know what else to do. She was all I had. We show up and this guy opens the door, all happy to see Jada, saying, Where you been lady, I missed you, and all that. He brings us in. We get high and it seems all right. We listen to music and watch TV with the sound off. They kiss a little bit, like no big deal. Then there's a knock on the door and a few guys come in. Jada seems cool and happy to see them, like they were buds from high school or something. So, you know, whatever. We sat around for a while, then Jada wanders off. I figure she's going to the bathroom or just moving around. You feel such crazy things in your body on meth. Then one guy gets up and then another. It all happens so slowly that I don't put it together. And then I'm sitting there with some other dude, looking into the bedroom, watching my sister get fucked by one guy, then another, and another. The guy across from me looks at me and nods and smiles. He gets up and goes into the room, unzipping his pants, but before he does anything, he says, 'What about the other one?' And they all turn and look. And I run, I fucking run. Out the door and down the street. I don't look back. My lungs were fire and my heart a machine gun. I was so terrified I couldn't stop if you put a wall in front of me. I don't even think they bothered to follow me. I ended up in a cemetery, way out in northeast. I fell to the ground and hid against some dead stone, looking all around me for the guys from the house. There was no sound but my heartbeat and my breath. I was there for hours, waiting for those fuckers, totally alert and ready. I had a rock in one hand and a vase in the other. The next thing I remember was the spade of a shovel tapping my foot. 'You can't be here, kid. We got a funeral.' That's what the guy holding the shovel said. Like nothing. Like every day he finds someone sleeping in the cemetery. Dead souls, Shrink, we're all dead souls."

What she told me was not anything I wanted to hear, not something I ever wanted to hear, and not something anyone should be made to endure. Women, girls, we're all too aware of our vulnerability. All the time. HG girls refuse to sublimate that vulnerability. I admire their actions, brutal as they are sometimes, and I hate that they're forced into those actions in the first place. Such is the ongoing nature of my work, though, when you think you've heard it all, or think you've heard all of the worst that one person has to tell, there's more. There's worse.

"I didn't try to stop them," she said. "I didn't call the police. I just ran. I'm a fucking coward. I have no idea where my sister is. My mom or my sister. Probably dead."

"You have a strong survival instinct. There's no way you would have been able to stop them."

"I didn't do *anything*."

"You can go easier on yourself. You can forgive yourself. No one deserves that violence nor even the threat of it. You're here now. Away from all that. You don't have to live that life."

"Easy for you to sit there and say."

"I mean it. You have choices. You can put that all behind you and let it go. Sit with it, feel it, yes, but don't live in it."

"Let it go? How the fuck do you do that? There's no such thing."

She was right. No one can drop that kind of guilt completely, just kiss it into the wind. They can only hold it within themselves, a stone on the shore, the tide wearing it down, but disappearing it would take eons.

"You said talking would help. It doesn't. Talking sucks. Talking brings everything right back and shoves it in your face again, down your throat, so you choke on it all over again. Doesn't do shit to change things."

We sat there, separately, together, in silence, in knowingness, alone. She would feel responsible for her sister for a lifetime. She would be stuck wondering. I felt sick and inadequate. I wanted to wrap her in my arms and hold her. Forever wouldn't be long enough.

Several days later, after several sessions of thick silence, Kyle asked, "You sick of me?"

"No, Kyle. I'm not sick of you. Quite the opposite, I like you very much. There's no tiring of you."

At some level just below the edge of consciousness, Kyle wanted all of my attention. Needed it. This person, the shrink, expert in human psychology. Kyle needed my rapt attention because that would confirm something fundamental for her —that she was someone worth studying, that she was fascinating and worthwhile. If the doctor in psychology withdrew attention, Kyle would regard that as tragic, devastating, because she'd find confirmation that she wasn't fascinating, that she wasn't worth even a shrink's time. Aware of this, true as it was for most of the girls, I acted accordingly. My job those days, most days, was mother, mentor, confidant, but most of all, my job was to take a genuine interest in Kyle until Kyle took that interest in herself. Most days, with most girls, I did this without effort because I saw into those girls. I saw the best in them and who they could become.

I could see her worry that she'd revealed too much. In response, I remained as calm and open as ever. I was on her side. The talking *did* help. She calmed down. She didn't pick fights. She never jumped from the roof again, nor harmed herself in other obvious ways, and she started to talk about other things. Her world admitted a sliver of possibility. Little by little the resistance to which the girls hold so firmly disintegrates.

"You married?" she asked one day, an outward shift.

"No, but I've been with the same woman for five years."

"Dude, so you've passed that happy fuck-fuck stage?"

I waited.

"Doesn't last, you know," she said. "You might stay together but the sex dies off, and talking about real things, it just all goes down the drain. I've seen it. Pretty soon you'll get fat and sit on the couch all day," she said, sagely. "I've seen my mom get excited about a new guy and three weeks later it's over. And my sisters, they're worse. They sit around watching TV all the time. It doesn't make any sense. But you're from a different world. Are you gonna make it? You think you'll be together when you're old and gray and out of your minds? Either you want it or you don't, and you have to want it bad for it to last. I hear the people in here, the parents, the staff. I overhear their shit. It's so good in the beginning and then everything goes all fucky. Passion deflates. People resign themselves. They settle. Shit gets in the way. I don't want that. That ain't the way to do it. I don't want to settle. That beginning gaga fuck-fuck crazy lust stuff is for kids. What counts is the love that comes after you've been through the worst together. When you know each other so fucking long and so fucking well. When you're past the point of being on the verge of splitting, past the cheating, or wanting to, past any drugs or booze or weird accidents, past the will-we-make-it thoughts and into 'Yeah, motherfucker, yeah.'"

Once you've opened these girls to questions, the next step is convincing them to keep questioning and once in a while find an answer, even a temporary one. The point is to value the questions. That way you can't go wrong. The sculptor Henry Moore said, "The secret of life is to have a task, something you devote your entire life to, something you bring everything to, every minute of the day for your whole life. And the most important thing is—it must be something you cannot possibly do!" My task is to help the girls find that thing, that flow, their bliss.

At some point a shift occurs. Suddenly, miraculously, inexplicably. Always resistance and compliance. A resident will share something so close, so awful, then retreat, defy, hide for days, weeks, longer, and then return. Time and again, I tried to take Kyle back to the meth house, the cemetery, hoping she would shift her thinking, relax her sense of complicity, and allow another story to emerge. She had more to relinquish, but I had to accept that she might not reveal more, or not to me. I try to turn the girls from their jungle paths into wide open fields.

On my way out the door on the Thursday before the fateful interlude, I came across Kyle sitting very still, by a window in the common room. I asked her what she was doing.

"Trying to be good."

I waited.

"You're gonna think it's silly. But I see myself in the country, living on a small farm. I'd have some animals like a horse and cow, or a pig and a dog, a mean and stupid dog. A chicken. I do like my scrambled eggs. All to myself, taking care of it all. I'd maybe have a few books around to read. Maybe be with a guy who works in the city and comes for long weekends. It'd be nice. Peaceful."

Sitting in the common room, wondering how to be good, wondering what that would mean. The simplicity of the idea combined with the trouble she had enacting it, told me a lot about the state of her mind. Follow rules. Stay out of trouble. Play fair. That was all. Imagine a future for yourself safely away from people. Following rules you didn't agree with was hard, and if you weren't following rules, you were in trouble. No staying out of it. But there Kyle was in slow, steady contemplation. Thought before action. Thinking of the future. Tending to animals and earth. There she was.

On Thursdays Alice went to yoga and then to a drumming circle while I completed case notes, planned for the upcoming week, and worked on a book about narrative psychology and the female teenager. That Thursday I had stalled out, and, taking a break, I went for walk. Turning off 21st onto Kearney, I saw Alice's bicycle locked outside the yoga studio which was dark and shut down for the night. Not knowing where she drummed, I didn't think anything of the abandoned bike. By chance I looked up. Above the studio, soft, wavering light showed through the curtains. Two figures stood close to one another, talking perhaps, until a hand reached to the other's face, the two lingered and looked, and then merged. I knew one of them. I knew her in silhouette, knew her a football field away, knew her next to me in flesh and flush.

I reached for my face, which was collapsing upon itself. My mind, my crowded head, became a thousand shattered thoughts. I stood in the still air, the still night. The lights in the other brick buildings were low or off. People were sleeping or dreaming or fucking, watching TV or reading or arguing. Doing what they do Thursday nights. They had no window into my mind, its sudden roaring chaos. I thought of Jung.

At the end, he wrote that his mind was a jungle of memories. Only memories. His mind was still functioning. But his memories were a jungle. The chaos spread to my body. My whole being burned, filled with predators and unsuspecting prey. I cooked into a blinding whiteness and I understood after so many years the white heat, the white light of beginnings and ends.

I stood there. Minutes? Hours? The whiteness dimmed. The lights above the studio were out, the figures unseen. I turned and walked home. I questioned what I'd seen. Had I imagined it? Was the figure Alice? Unmistakably. At her drum circle. Was there ever a circle?

I went to the home I could no longer call home. I tore the sheets from the bed that was no longer our bed. I hurled candles at the walls. I opened cupboards and swept them of their contents. Anything I could lift I threw into the chaos. I threw dining room table chairs into the hall. I threw her clothes, her artwork, her books, her pottery, her drums, her albums, her oils down the stairs. I trashed everything except my own desk and research. Somehow I had sense enough to keep my work intact. I stomped around and slammed doors. I screamed. And then I left. I could no longer stay in my own residence, even after exhausting myself through destruction. Spent and empty, I couldn't get a deep breath. I couldn't go to a bar or visit a friend because I didn't want to be around anyone. Most of all I didn't want to be around when Alice returned scented by another. I got into my car and drove past the last of the city lights, past the little comfort those lights offered, drove out along the dark two-lane highway into the country toward the coast where black water pooled on the right. A deeper feeling of exhaustion came over me, one that follows exertion, tears, lack of sleep, and an angry head. My survival instincts took control, turning the car and wending the roads to her family's cottage. I found the hidden key and opened the door, lit a fire. Welcome, said the drafts and shadows and memories. Outside, the black water continued its rhythms, unconcerned that I was there.

I must have slept. The fire was out when I woke. I shivered against everything. I rekindled the flames, which glowed indifferently. Coming to the cottage was a mistake. Nothing in it belonged to me. The blankets and board games. The pictures and projects. All hers and her family's. My family was twenty-five hundred miles away, ignorant of the fact they'd never see their assumed daughter-in-law again. Two Thanksgivings, three Christmases, a summer visit. My parents had liked Alice immediately, her warm demeanor, her generous spirit. Full blue eyes. She laughed readily and took them in. Fucking Alice off fucking someone else. On the shelf of her family's cottage, where I trespassed, was a book I'd long forgotten I'd left there. I sat in the musty recliner, the same recliner I'd knelt before and nestled my face between Alice's skinny legs. I flipped the pages and tried to lose myself in the theory of optimal experience.

I stayed in that mistake until Sunday.

Once home, the phone wouldn't stop ringing, and would go on sounding off, I suspected, all evening, until I picked up. I silenced the ringer and continued my post-coast plan, which involved sitting or lying on the sofa and staring off, not thinking or feeling a thing, if I could only somehow manage that. I couldn't. Alice was all around me. I began to ache. Only three days and already I missed the lovely, lonely banal moments, the trivial daily acts witnessed by another. Standing at the sink, brushing, flossing, not talking. Making oatmeal, coffee in the morning, reading the paper across the table. Meaning derived from shared trivia. Because someone cared, the mundane took on worth because someone witnessed it, even peripherally.

When I was a child, I presumed that God was watching. I was never alone and always being judged. This was the beginning of my exhibitionism and its opposite, voyeurism. The girls at The Garden had the same problem, always being watched. Never alone. Physically. Slumped on the sofa, alone, the sky going dark, I envied them this. I wanted someone to watch me. We didn't have to talk or touch or interact at all. I just wanted that potential wrapped in separateness.

I lifted the incessant phone to my ear. "Don't you dare hang up," Meghan said. "Get dressed. You're coming to dinner with us."

"I am dressed and I can't. I have things."

"You know better than to try this with me. I'm too stubborn and I know you too well. I will come over there and drag your ass out."

I sighed. "You shouldn't have called the work line."

"You're not answering your home line. There was no other way to get through."

"Because I'm working. On my book."

"I don't believe you. I know something's up and I will find out what it is. We're picking you up in twenty minutes. I don't care what you say."

Meghan, relentless Meghan, and Remmy, her wife of seven years. Both writers, Meghan a journalist, and Remmy a poet-turned-fiction-writer, who talked endlessly about words, semantics. They corrected pronunciation and grammatical errors on menus and billboards, anywhere, everywhere. Their flirty game used to amuse me. Meghan and Remmy's courtship was a consequence of an assignment. Meghan had to profile Katharine Remson for the local personality pages of the weekly paper. They read Rilke and Rossetti aloud to each other within earshot of me. During that time Meghan, who'd been kicked out of her previous tenancy, was staying at my place. I could still recite lines from "The Goblin Market,"

> *Did you miss me?*
> *Come and kiss me.*
> *Never mind my bruises...*

"The Market," a text you must read to be a literate lesbian. The romanticism of reading, of them, sharpened my mouth with a metallic taste. In softer moments, I remembered Meg and Remmy's brief courtship fondly, going with Meghan to a four-story bookstore where shelves reached from the floor and met ceilings. Books, crowded spine to spine, spilled onto the carpet. Meg was in search of obscure quotes and images that she would copy to a postcards and leave beneath Remmy's pillow. All so fucking romantic. While Meghan dug through piles of water-stained hardbacks, I read Jung's collected works. Eighty-one when he wrote *Memories, Dreams, Reflections*, his own biography. Suspect in and of itself because as Leibovitz once said, you should never write your own biography. If your life is worth one, someone else will do it for you. And suspect because what you remember is rarely what you experienced or witnessed. Lies, all lies. That's what memory is.

For as much as Meg and Rem loved language, its proper use and arcane words, they'd somehow both developed the inability, or had forgotten or blotted out the simple one-letter word: I. They'd become a unit. Decisions, ideas, feelings, everything came from the plural, united we. We. We. We. The point was they, taken together, and they were always together, were intolerable and inseparable. Which partially explains my not returning phone calls and not answering the door during unannounced drop-ins. My disdain for this type of codependent coupling may also partly explain my failed relationships. Perhaps I'm too independent and aloof. Too much I.

"Just the soup and salad, please," I told the server, thinking of Kelly, who would have ordered big. No matter her mood, who died, what country had been bombed, who left, she could always eat. Not me. My stomach clamped down in times of distress.

"Dressing?"

"No dressing."

"Get something else," Meghan said. "It's on me." Two years prior, Meghan had become a silent partner in the restaurant. Her twin brother, Paul, the manager and other owner, cashed out of a law firm and bought the struggling bar, turning a rare profit in the first year of business. In the bar, an elegant, spacious design of dark bamboo floors and walls of deep reds, I felt calm.

"I'm fine with the salad."

"Where have you been all weekend?" Rem asked. "We expected you at my reading Friday night."

"You can't keep shutting us out," Meghan said.

Let's take bets, I thought. I hadn't been shutting them out, letting the friendship lapse, per se. I was just busy. Work and writing and running. Days didn't have enough hours for poetry readings. "It's not personal," I'd told her—them, on several occasions when she and Remmy and Alice had dragged me out. That week, though, was different. I told them, briefly, what had happened, ending it with, "I'm pretty sure we're breaking up."

"Pretty sure?"

"Fucking others being deal-breakers and all."

"You haven't talked to her?"

"I don't need to."

The two of them stared at me as I crunched lettuce.

"Five years is nothing to shake a stick at. You're in. Work it out," Meghan said. "People give up all too easily these days. They change jobs, cars, houses, trade in husbands and wives as if returning a shirt at a department store. No one has any staying power."

"I don't disagree," I said.

"But?"

I shrugged.

"You're such a bull."

We sat, chewing away at our meals. If you keep quiet long enough, others are bound to speak. Few people can sit quietly for very long. Remmy broke in, "Well, if you're decided, why don't you take up yoga or some other rebalancing activity?

Studios are popping up all over the place. I'm sure you could find a cheap package."

"Yoga? You want me to take up yoga?"

"Weren't you and Alice always discussing being more active together? I think you should do it without her. On your own."

"That's what you got from what I just said?"

Remmy nodded emphatically. "A healthy way to pass the time."

"You think it'd be good for me."

"Well, sure."

"For a writer you have such shitty footing when it comes to emotion and motive and subtext." Remmy penned lesbian romance novels, not the types of books you had to read to be a literate lesbian. "Yoga," I sneered, about to say more.

Meghan cut me off, "Stop it, Lee. She's trying to help." For as close as they were, Meghan still understood me better.

"It's fine," I said. "Can we move on to something else?"

"Rem and I were talking about something earlier. Does the soul become a self through life experience or is the brain a machine and the self just results from spectacular brain activity?"

"That's consoling," I said.

"Don't be mean."

"Either version doesn't make life any less meaningful," Remmy said.

"Doesn't it?" I said. "Consciousness is a black box in the psych world. The behaviorist world."

"And your world?"

"That whole world of thought, that we're all just bags of neurons, doesn't address the base fact that I'm aware my neurons are firing and that I'm thinking and feeling exactly what I'm thinking and feeling," Meghan said.

"That's what I'm saying," Remmy again. "Whether the self evolves from experience or nervous activity, without consciousness there is no story. A happening is inseparable from its observation. The tree doesn't fall in the forest if you're not there."

"The hell it doesn't," I said.

"You have to agree, working where you do, seeing what you do. I mean, isn't that what your book is building toward? The idea that consciousness is the meaning of life? Even if you don't outright say it in that way. Your new therapy is based on this, right?"

"No, no, no, no, no. There is no new therapy. It's impossible. That's funny, though, years ago my analyst used to tease me that I was trying to reinvent psychotherapy. She'd say, 'The wheel is already here, use it.'" Meg knew what to ask to fire me up, get me outside of my particular neurotic miscarriages, and for a brief moment I had a hold on things and thought everything would be okay. I'd return to work Monday, ready to confront the aftermath of my brief absence, and work the girls into better lives. "Then after more talk, Maud would say the opposite of something she'd said vehemently only moments before. It was pretty confusing at the time."

"It's the same with literature, there being nothing new. No new stories, just different versions of the original seven. Lust, envy, greed."

"Those are deadly sins," I said. Meghan was goading me, but I played along. "There are only four stories. The love story, the struggle for power, the journey, and the various combinations of these."

"A yoga instructor," Remmy, not listening, in her own world, mused. "Imagine the sex they're having. Deep breathing. Tantric."

For a brief moment, I'd been fine. "Fuck you, Rem. That's just rude." I popped up from my seat. "I'm going home."

Meghan grabbed my arm. "Don't. Rem's done. Aren't you?" she said pointedly, glaring at her, then whispered, "She never talks about her book. You know that's a good sign."

"You never could whisper well."

"C'mon, Lee, sit down."

"Yeah, please. I'm sorry. Tell us more."

"There's no getting back on track now," I said. Remmy had steered me into a memory of Alice and me, both naked, sitting upright and entwined, Alice in my lap, her legs wrapped around me. She'd had us doing a breathing exercise that supposedly synced our rhythms and charged our root chakras. I remained in the pose for an eternal seven minutes. Alice had been gently rocking and her movement teased me into a frenetic energy that I unleashed by flipping her on her back and exploding her root chakra.

"Isn't it better to talk these things out? Aren't you always saying that?"

"Yeah, it is better. I know the theory and all the jargon and that I need the support of my friends at times like these, but mutherfuck, can't you just let me be for a day? I'll come to you when I'm ready."

"Obviously we can't because you won't come to us. You've never done that, and I doubt you ever will."

"So? We're all fine in the end."

"That's not friendship, Lee. That's convenience and a warm body nearby."

"Talk to us about something, then, anything," Remmy said.

"What? So you can take notes, scrape at my shitty life, and I can see it show up in a crappy romance novel?"

"You know what?" Remmy said. "*I'll* go home. I love you to death, but you're intolerable right now. I mean, c'mon, it's not like you were together for twenty years."

"Oh, so duration equals depth?"

"She isn't trying to minimize your feelings."

"For not trying, she's a fucking expert. Stop defending her. She has hit every raw nerve I have."

"All you have are raw nerves."

"I'll go," Remmy said.

I exhaled, relieved and surprised. I sat for some seconds in silence with Meghan, before saying, "You know who I was thinking about earlier?"

She waited.

"Sam."

"You're not trying that again."

"What about Paul? You know I've always had a crush on him." Lean, boyish Paul in his late forties with deep-set alert eyes.

"He's my brother, my *twin* brother."

"He's much taller. Is he seeing anyone?"

"You know he never tells me those things."

Almost six years ago now, Paul's wife, Christine, died from cancer. Paul had all but stopped eating and was rail thin, as if he were the one afflicted. I remembered patiently listening to him and alternately trying to rush him to sober up in the months after Christine died. He could do nothing but drink and talk and drink and talk, pounding his fists on the closest surface or tearing at his unkempt hair. "Her beautiful breasts were full of disease. Who knows for how many years? How many times I ran my hands over them, adored them, kissed them. All the while, angry, gray nodules were laughing at me. Mocking. Their laughter getting louder as they burrowed and crawled and grew bigger until one day they said, 'Fuck your adoration, Paul. Watch what we do to your wife now.' Did you know she had breast cancer in her family? Her grand-mother and aunt. I didn't know until her mother told me after the funeral. She never went to the doctor. She was always so busy with campaigns and actions. I would have made her go to the doctor. Once. One time would have made all the dif-ference." He didn't stop talking, and he didn't stop drinking for five months. Shortly after that he planted himself on the counter behind the bar and has been there since. "She was the ambitious one," he told me. "She wanted to change the world. Would have. This state would have universal healthcare by now if she were still alive. And you know, as I am now? She would never marry the man I am now."

"Where is he, anyway? He never leaves the bar when it's open."

Meghan looked toward the counter where Paul usually sat behind the bar, aimlessly, kicking his long legs, reading a book. "Beats me," she said. "Look, seriously, what are you going to do?"

I shrugged.

"I know you. You're going to have to do something."

"What are you talking about?"

"Your tailspins. You and the ends of relationships don't play well together. We've known each other nearly a decade now. Do you remember how we met?"

"Someone's dinner party."

"A sex party at the Queen of Hearts."

"You'd never go to a sex party."

"I was writing a story for the weekly, trying to get my foot in the door. We both stood outside one of those filthy rooms watching your girlfriend watch a man get fucked by two women."

"Kelly." I smiled at the memory of Kelly.

"You weren't smiling then. You were pissed. You didn't want to be there. I didn't either. Three in the morning and we went to that shithole pancake house by the bridge."

"They've remodeled. It's very nice now."

"My point is, you two fought and fought and broke up but continued sleeping together for months. You couldn't be adults and just part ways."

"Nobody does that. Nobody shakes hands and says 'I wish you the best in your life. I really enjoyed my time with you.'"

"Sam did. Kris did."

"Yeah, and it annoyed the shit out of me."

"You see my point?"

"Kelly was great."

"Your world upends when things end. I don't want to have to remind you about Mignon, and you've been with Alice the longest."

Slinky, smoldering Mignon. "I miss Mignon. Kris was the longest."

"By your own admission you were a kid. This is exactly what you do. Things end horribly and you conveniently erase all the bad bits."

"It's a strategy." I didn't have the energy to argue.

"Looks like something serious is going on here. No Katharine? No Alice? It's got to be bad." The only one to call Remmy by her full, first name, Paul squeezed my shoulder and kissed his sister on the cheek. "Have a drink at the bar," he said.

Meghan sighed. "I've gotta check on Remmy. Talk some sense into this one," she said, thumbing at me.

I followed Paul to the bar. "You never take time off," I said. "How about a scotch?"

"Left Brian in charge." He passed me a drink after two quick pours.

"That's not scotch. Too light to be scotch. You're not going to make any friends that way."

"Friends are overrated."

"Explain that to your sister."

Paul asked few questions, yet was aware of the world around him. I liked that about him. And he didn't mind silence. Certain types of sad people don't mind silence. They prefer it. For others, silence is death; they require noise. I don't understand those types. In a graceful lift, Paul was on the counter, kicking his legs, eying me suspiciously. "Don't take my crossword."

"Brian? Seriously, on a night like this?"

"The one and only."

"And you're okay with that?"

"He needs to redeem himself."

"He stole a thousand dollars worth of booze. You had to replace your dishes and glasses because he trashed the kitchen. Why do *you* have to redeem him?"

"I'm surprised to hear this from you."

So was I. I touted forgiveness and tough love with the girls. Touted the unlimited capacity for growth. Growth, not change. Change is inevitable. Growth falls along the positive side of the spectrum.

"He's doing some fine work. And I don't mean in the kitchen. His art. When you were in last week I don't think you noticed the walls."

"Is he back in school?"

"He's exploring the notion that you can do art for a living. Live in the gap between art and life."

"So he's doomed?"

"Yes."

"And you're going to stand by and watch him crash again? What does that mean, anyway? The gap between art and life."

"According to Brian it has something to do with living from the inside out."

"Heart on your sleeve?"

"It's not for all of us."

"Alice is gone," I said, knowing he wouldn't ask.

"There are consolations, you know. Do you want the clichés? The helpful aphorisms? I know them all. I have lists upon lists."

"Tell me the ones that work."

He wiped at the counter with a microfiber cloth.

"I assume you had a date," I said. "I know you have your share."

"They feel sorry for me."

"A lay is a lay is a lay. Even when it's a pity lay. Sometimes those are the best kind. They work a little harder. Is it serious?"

"I'm the type of guy who likes a strong woman. A woman who wants to do things. But those types of women usually need a man who can match them. I'm a barnacle. I hang on to the ship that's going places so I don't have to propel myself."

"There's a psychologist who revised a Plato myth. He says before we were born we chose a template, an idea of ourselves, that we'll live out on earth. Our bodies, our parents, our troubles, our destinies. But we don't know this, or don't remember because we run through the field of Lethe right before conception. Of all things, you chose to be a barnacle?"

"Meghan talking about consciousness again?"

"It's her latest story, isn't it? Rag journalists learn a little about a lot."

"Sounds like I made some bad selections before running through that field," Paul said.

"Like songs in a jukebox."

"May as well be."

"People who lead unhappy lives are cut off from their original story. I was going to use that somehow in my book. Everything comes back to narrative. We've forgotten our capital-s story. I was thinking about how I always tell the girls you've got to go back before you can go forward. You've got to understand the past before you can create a new future. Tell the old story to enable yourself to create a new one. But maybe it's not quite that, maybe it's not about creating a new story but it's about connecting with *The* Story."

"The best shrinks have the most fucked-up lives."

"You teach what you most need to learn."

Paul said, "All right, I've got one. I'm under a circus tent. I'm the woman who does tricks on the backs of elephants.

Though in the dream, I'm not a woman. I'm me and the crowd loves me. Then it shifts and I'm in a cage, staring into the mouth of a drooling tiger, like I've failed in taming it."

"Wish fulfillment mixed with death anxiety."

"That's it?"

"You're the bartender. You're supposed to be listening to me."

"You're not talking about your troubles."

"That's why we get along so well," I said.

"I haven't remembered a dream in over a week." I had a few fragments, but they were a blur. I usually remembered my dreams. They presented clearly, the movie of my soul in crisp colors. I used to love dreaming, dreams. Hearing other's recount theirs. Recalling my own. Asking Alice what she remembered from her sleep. Dreams were the language of the gods. The short road to the unconscious. The mind's making sense of the day. The indy, art-film of the individual. Last trace of originality. And I couldn't remember. My unconscious, blocked, pushed nothing through the barriers.

"Impossible."

"I know."

In a college paper I'd argued that the value of dreams was as a tool to advance the dialogue in therapy sessions. So-called correct interpretation was inconsequential. Dreams in group sessions were a point from which associations and interpretations issued forth. The role of dreams elsewhere was another matter entirely. They were wish fulfillment. They were messages from the collective unconscious; astrological guides, event predictors; they were the mind's reckoning the waking life. In turn, each of these and more. I read Freud's seminal work once a year. Then followed it with Jung's papers on dreams, excerpted from his collected works. I read everything I could. Any newly published book, including the pop-psychology manuals and astrologers' pamphlets. Alongside my dream log, as best I could, I kept a detailed list of all the dreams anyone has ever told me.

"I'll tell you what," I told Paul. "Eliot was wrong about April. Dead fucking wrong."

"You're being unnecessarily morose for a Sunday night."

"'Something in a Sunday,'" I sang. "It's too bad you're not a woman."

He lifted an eyebrow.

"Can I have another drink now?" Then I told him about being chased through the jungle by some kind of tribe who was going to kill me if they caught me. My sister was there, running with me and she got caught and I couldn't leave her to them so I slowed and let them take me. They put us up on the roof of a tall building where we were made to walk the outer edge. There was no ladder, no escape. I knew we going to be killed. At the next corner I broke from the line and I sprinted diagonally to the other corner and lept from the edge, suddenly bursting into flight with these huge, flapping wings. Free. "That was my first entry in the journal and it wasn't even my dream. It was Hailey's. The first twenty are. I always wanted it to have been my dream. But they were all Hailey's back then. She was nuts. She really was free. And she left me behind." I shook my empty glass at Paul.

"I think of it differently now," he said, "when other people leave. Their leaving has nothing to do with us. Nothing whatsoever. It has everything to do with them." He stood, reaching his lanky frame toward the tall ceiling. With that reach I saw him as a young man. A young man with the kind of good looks and gentleman's demeanor that made his friend's mothers at first wish he were their son and then be grateful he wasn't, as they imagined secreting him off to an overpriced hotel. "What do you think she's doing now? Hailey."

"If she's not dead from a heroin overdose, she's making people pay attention in some strange way or another. Teaching art to convicts or crack addicts. That's the trick, you know. To be alive in the world."

"Good story, but I'm still not pouring you scotch. You wouldn't like it."

"You'd pour for some nameless jerk."

I looked over at Paul, sitting on the counter, kicking his legs. He looked good, freshly laid. His skin had a healthy, vibrant glow. He was calm, assured. Hard to imagine him any other way. He'd been heavy when I first met him, bearish, from the thickening into marriage, into middle age, from steak and martini lunches and practicing law in a high-powered firm. But then he turned. He shrugged. One minute he bordered at the edge of seven figures, the next he didn't. He bought the bar and shed his previous life. Simple, outwardly.

"Who is it this week?" I asked.

"Hesse."

Since taking over the bar, Paul had become a dedicated reader, selecting a writer, then moving chronologically through everything that writer had written, minor works and memoirs included.

"One of my profs had a thing for Hesse. When he saw me reading *Steppenwolf* he told me because I was a girl I needn't bother and if I was going to be stubborn enough to read it anyway then I should wait, as Hesse implies in the introduction, until I was older."

"And?"

"Well, the professor was an arrogant prick so I read it and didn't understand it. Then read it again in my thirties and still didn't understand it."

"This won't help," he said, finally pouring me another drink.

There was no panacea for anger, for loneliness, for being alone. Paul knew this much more than I did. The lover having left. The grand shift. The gaping hole. Tears, quickly pursued by angry thoughts. *Why are you crying? You shouldn't be fucking crying. You're too old to be crying like this. You should know better.* My face, a riot of emotion. I slugged the drink.

Outside, the air was cool and damp. The gray sky indifferent. The black trees made blacker, velvety with the wet. Saturated, fat, bare trees. I took a few, slow, deep breaths of the cold air, which burned through my nostrils. I reached down to touch my toes, pulling at the tight holds in my body. Gradually, the muscles and connective tissues slackened, giving way to gravity, and my body folded, my head and arms dropping closer to the ground. I inhaled, counting to eight. It wasn't yoga. I wasn't practicing yoga. Not ever yoga. At one a.m., with a buzz blurring the day and a residue of anger, I walked home. With each step, I tried to bully myself out of the sour mood that comes after drinking. I wondered what the others would do, and with this thought, I allowed myself the slightest smile. My own immodesty, the subtle ingratiating of myself into the hall of heavy psychological thinkers. Sigmund, Carl, Carl again,

Rollo, and Anna who was surreptitiously analyzed by her own father and soon after admitted to the psychoanalytic institute. Anna, loyal to her father, loyal to the bitter cancer-lipped end. I was no Anna. My own father, no Sigmund. His analysis? "Buck up, kid. Get a job that gets you out of your head *and* other people's heads."

Or Maud.

Maud might say, "You have to stare at the thing itself until you understand it. Your gaze must be unwavering."

She might say, "You can sublimate these feelings. Use the anger to get work done."

She might say, "Some psyches are beyond access by conventional talk treatment. They require heavy, but careful medicating."

She might tell me to return to analysis. I'd been analyzed. Five full years, four hours weekly. Maud was a relic even then. She's got to be dead by now. I doubted analysis would work. I wanted a quick fix and was attempting that by drinking. My mind wound up and reeled and I couldn't control it. Maybe a high dose of a psychotropic, some psilocybin and a flight of religious fancy. I thought of the thousands of doctors who wanted to be strict Freudians, but the ease and perks of pharmacology kept getting in the way.

I put my hand to my head and tugged at the short stalks. I should have been better at self-consolation. Easier on myself. All those years of higher training. All that theory. The years of my own analysis. The upraising of others. I was dispirited. Wearied by my own thoughts. *You should have seen it coming. You did see it coming and you blatantly ignored it. You fucking idiot. You should have done something. You brought this on yourself.*

The shoulds. Should. That funny word of social, moral obligation, of expectation or probability. The auxiliary verb that shouldn't be because all the shoulds in the world won't help when someone doesn't act, can't act. "People should all over themselves all the time," my grandmother said in defense of whatever choice she was making, leaving her third husband for the third time, not going to the doctor to have a small lump in her abdomen checked. "You shouldn't ever do anything that you don't want to do. It's that simple." And then, "Shice!" when she jabbed her finger with the knitting needle. She loved those SH sounds. And when she did finally see a doctor who advised surgery and drugs and all sorts of expert things she had no use for, she said, "You make the decisions for your life, mister, and I'll make the decisions for mine." She lived four years past the doctor's expiration date. I wished my grandmother were still alive to tell me some anecdote, some bit of advice. My grandmother would never have been in this position. She was always the one doing the leaving.

The loft was in shambles. Yet, less so. Despite the detritus, the space felt hollow, as if uninhabited for weeks, except for the remnants of some other woman's life. I noticed why it felt hollow. The glass has been swept from the floor, and Alice's belongings were missing. And of all things, the bed, made. The sheets tucked tightly at the corners. Pillows fluffed. I scanned the cases for chocolates, as if a hotel maid had been through. But no, Alice must have come in, hurriedly straightened what she could, put clean sheets on the bed, clearing the slate, and taken her things while I was out. I cursed her for this and the great disappearing act and berated myself into the bathroom where I leaned on the sink and let the strong porcelain hold me up as the self-loathing tried to take me down. I was keenly aware that there were worse things that could be happening—cancer, early-onset Alzheimer's, AIDS, any of the basal ganglia disorders, not to mention any of the things Harrington girls face or have faced. And then there were famine, homelessness, and the distant epidemics to consider. Yet somehow nothing canceled what I hated most of all—self-pity. Self-loathing, on the other hand, I could accept. With loathing there's energy, something to work with. Loathing was palpable and shapely, massive and well-formed. Meaty. Pity dropped into itself—a bottomless chasm with no footholds or handholds for miles.

But that was just it, wasn't it? I *shouldn't* have to feel, either. I didn't have to, and besides, I didn't have time for the mess of a person I'd become after abandonment. I didn't want to cry or be pissed off or be hurt or vulnerable. Grieve? Follow the five stages? I was better than that. I didn't want to obey a program and shouldn't have to. Where did that land my grandmother? Particles scattered at the beach. Ashes in the sand. The woman had another ten years in her, solid ones, with a mind like hers. She *should* have consulted a physician sooner and followed his advice. But she was stubborn. She wasn't one to correct for the body's failings. Wasn't one to let mind power over matter. "When the body wants to go, you get out of the way. You let it go." But this wasn't about the body. This was about the mind, and keeping it, and keeping it intact, a feat I wasn't convinced was possible. Looking away from the mirror I saw tufts of gray in the corner and gathered in small, wettish clumps near the porcelain bases of the sink, the toilet, the tub. When was the last time I'd cleaned? Alice, having higher, more rigid standards usually took care of the bathroom.

Alice.

I didn't want to think about Alice.

Five years rounding toward six.

Didn't want to think about the fact of her so recently in the loft. The scent of her. The shape causing a change in airflow.

And why not? Wasn't that the quickest method of exorcism? Think her right out of the way. Wasn't that precisely what I was trained in helping others do? Help them move toward catharsis and insight? Why didn't I talk to someone, even a friend? Because it didn't help and I was as obstinate as my grandmother. The knowledge that others have survived similar trials didn't help. "We each feel our own pain in our very own ways," I mocked myself, rubbing my red-rimmed eyes. I tried to gather up my mind and body. I took in a deep breath. Again with the fucking breathing. Alice, always trying to get me to breathe. "Take the air down into your belly. Chest breaths only keep your shoulders tight. You can't relax fully, breathing the way you breathe."

Exasperated, I shook her voice from my head. "Fine," I said aloud to no one. To my grandmother. To Meghan. To myself. "I'll do it. I've got to do something. I'll process in some way. The five stages. I'll go through the five stages. A little self-help, pop-psych can't hurt." I separated my feet and stood firmly before the mirror, slowly pulling my arms and hands away from the sink.

One, Denial: Nope, this isn't happening. She'll come home tonight and prove to me that she wasn't the figure in the window.

Two, Anger: Fuck you for doing this to me, and fuck me for allowing you to do this to me.

Three, Bargaining: Please come back, baby. I'll be better. I'll be more attentive. I won't work so much. I'll cut back on running.

Four, Depression: I don't care. It doesn't matter. Nothing at all matters.

Five, Acceptance: She's gone. We had some good times and now we're over.

The stages for dealing with death. Applicable. We hadn't seen each other or talked. She left no note. No number nor forwarding information. She may as well have been dead. Cancel her license. Close her library and bank cards. My life with Alice would recede and I'd go on with my own life, perhaps with more abandon and devotion. I could stop worrying about growing old with her, growing deeper into our differences. I told myself I'd begin to think of her abstractly like a character in a book or film, one you feel unsure of, but can't forget, and not as someone who'd lie naked next to you and poke you with her toes, before rolling on top, whispering in your ear, "Make me come just like that again." I'd finally have all the time I wanted to work on my book. To work extra hours at The Garden. Implement new programs. Try new ideas. Follow-up on the girls who've passed through. Have the others return as visitors to tell the new, troubled girls the new untroubled stories they've created. Yes, I could finally do, unreservedly, the work I'd been called to do. I'd lose myself in this, for wasn't that one of life's sweet consolations? To get lost in your work. I'd come to think fondly of that woman I once lived with for a few years those many years ago. Simple. Just that simple.

Fantasies, all.

The task, as if it were a trivial chore like emptying the dishwasher or taking the car in for an oil change, and not what was my life's work, what I had devoted myself to. I saw what I wanted to do, what I wanted for the girls, but there, right there, was the paradox. What I wanted: irrelevant. The girls had their own lives to lead. I had been so successful in keeping this fact hidden from myself. And that, I was finding out wasn't an inkling of the myriad other hidden things.

First the empty bed.

Last the empty bed.

Home from dinner, drinks, from my blitzkrieg of a weekend, sober again and wide awake, I walked out of the bathroom and ripped off my clothes and put on running clothes. In the spare room, I punched the keys on the treadmill that entered me in a three a.m. 10K cross-country race against my anger and irritation, a race to see who would win: exhaustion or emotion. I was intent on running out the day. Running away.

"Lee."

I jumped. I whipped around toward the bed, barely catching myself on the handrails of the treadmill. My heart pounded against my throat. Alice's soft face emerged from beneath the covers of the bed.

"I was here the other day, but you weren't. I thought maybe you had a conference I'd forgotten about, but that didn't make sense once I saw the mess. I wanted to explain. I'd been reaching for you for months. I think I see now that my explanations won't matter to you. I was going to leave my key. I guess I fell asleep. Still, I tried to talk to you. I wanted us to see some-one or go somewhere. Together. I wanted this to work. Us to work. I tried. You were so unavailable." She paused, but continued to gaze at me with her benign eyes. "A thought keeps going through my head. Something you said a while ago about the girls, about everyone, that if they didn't get it at home, they'd look for it elsewhere. It's a true statement. I didn't want it to be this way, but Jac—"

"I don't want to know. I don't want details. Just get the rest of your belongings. I don't want any part of you here when I get back."

"We should talk, Lee. You of all people, where are you go-ing?"

There are people who can withstand conflict.

There are people who can yell and carry on.

There are people who can talk, who have to talk.

There are people who argue for hours.

People who resolve differences and come to stalemates by talking incessantly.

People who clutch and cry.

People who somehow remain friends after intimacy ends.

People who after their third wives leave them pick up a ma-chete and head off to elementary schools.

I got back in the car.

Betrayal, like anyone's death and the grief the living carry, is familiar. All too familiar.

My words wouldn't matter.

Alice's explanations wouldn't matter.

Justifications are fatwood to a fired mind.

I skipped work Monday. I haven't called out in seven years, as you know. Seven whole years, and not one unplanned absence. There was an illness in the family, I lied, knowing I was undoing months of work with the girls. Because of my unplanned and unexplained absence their trust would disintegrate. I had also undone months of momentum on the book. The brown desk at the kitchen window collected dust from days of disuse. And I had undone the strength and endurance I'd built in my body, training for an ultramarathon. My muscles and self-discipline already atrophying. I couldn't sleep. I couldn't eat. I was one large cliché and I didn't care. And I was someone who cared. Someone who gave a damn. I gave a damn about my work, my friends, my bills, my loft. I gave a damn about global warming, local politics, recycling. I gave a damn about longevity and cholesterol levels and staying fit, eating organic. I gave a damn about children's television-watching habits, about plastic containers leaching chemicals, about battered women and homeless men. I gave a damn about conflict in the Middle East, in Russia, in the inner cities of America, about adolescent girls on the verge of destroying their lives before their lives had even begun. I gave a damn.

And then I didn't. One incident, and I completely upended my life, layered chaos upon chaos. You see? Even now I'm quick to unravel. My mind takes me places beyond my control, places I don't want to be. Digression after digression. Meghan was right. I go a little nutty when things end, when people leave.

As I returned to the car Sunday night, I noticed the book from the cottage on the seat beside me. I committed to a mission: bring order to chaos, lift the subliminal to the conscious.

Flow. Go forward to go back. Remedy the past with experiences from the present. The two contradicted one another, I knew. Go forward. Be here now. I was Whitman: riddled with contradictions.

In the Redwoods I thought of possibility and impossibility. Three-hundred-seventy-foot trees, impossibly massive and old and everywhere in sight, glowered over me tucked up tight in my bag and tent. Two days back, Portland's October sky, packed with clouds and memories, were suffocating me. I had sense to chase the sun. I drove south on my paradoxical errand, down I-5 through Salem and hippie Eugene, cutting west from Grants Pass toward the water and then south into the woods. I walked among those giants for five hours, watching light and fog play dirty tricks with their branches. I attended to the present tense and studied fine lines of long bark, and felt my feet on the damp, hollow-sounding earth.

I couldn't motivate myself to run. Running is something I usually love, after the first twenty minutes, anyway, pushing my body through stiffness into speed, sprinting up a hill, cresting with the feeling that I'd swallowed fire. Last year I upped my distance, enduring more. Maybe aging impelled me. Maybe the sediment of monotony. I'd run the Portland Marathon, another in Vancouver. Both times I survived without injury and ran the next day. Six weeks ago, training for the JFK50 in November, I logged twenty-eight miles on Saturday and another dozen on Sunday, a nightcap of sorts. The

JFK50, originally part of Kennedy's fitness push for the country, adapted a Roosevelt requirement for officers to cover fifty miles on foot in twenty hours. If the officers didn't make it, they relinquished their commissions. The Kennedy Challenge evolved into a memorial run after Kennedy's assassination. I didn't want to run with the granola racers of the Western States 100 or Leadville. I wanted to compete on the opposite coast with military elite. So much for that.

Thirty-five is not old, only halfway to death by biblical accounting, but excessive running might be manifestation of death anxiety. And what better way to ward off my own death than by memorializing another's life? Kennedy, the thirty-fifth president, my thirty-fifth year. Thirty-five is half of seventy, which both my grandmothers didn't pass. I'd arrived at my midlife crisis, and mad-dashed from the exploratory anatomy slab where I'd gingerly sliced the dead epidermis into two wide flaps and one by one removed the organs. Soon enough impatience overcame fear and I tossed the appendix in with the livers, spleens in with the stomachs. The heart and all of its aches, its adhesions, given barely a glance, weighed and thumbed and dropped in the bucket of hearts for others to dice. And in the end—incineration. Ashes, all. In light of this, running makes sense. Technical trudges up McKinley make sense. So, too, swimming with sharks and downing whiskey, needling veins and base-jumping. Rage, rage.

All of these deviant activities appear pointless, inefficient. There's no logic to be found in spending hours in sour sneakers and knee, hip, or foot pain, complete bodily exhaustion. These activities are good for nothing, certainly not the public good. What are they about? Effort. What's important isn't anything visible or tangible, only what you feel, what you endure. A different self-awareness, a new shade of understanding what you are emerges. Tame by comparison, the running. I'm not an adrenaline junkie nor a Transcendentalist. I'm not a kid fleeing to Alaska. I couldn't camp in a bus or kill a moose. One of the girls talked about an aunt who canoed six hundred miles from Prudhoe Bay to Fairbanks. Not me. I'm not an adventurer, not a climber nor skier. Sixty pounds in a nylon duffel strapped on my hips and shoulders is not my idea of a vacation. Camping in the Redwoods in a tent with my car nearby is enough wilderness fun for me. Still, in the forest I found myself thinking I could snuggle with a protest chain against the bark, shit in a bucket, sleep in a sling, to save even one of those giant red beasts, if I had to. If I'd lived a different life. If I'd been raised differently.

Later, shivering in my tent, I shivered not only against the cold, but also against the impossibility, the absurdity, of being alive in the world, of being human. Alone in the tent, in the damp, sudden shock of existential awareness, I twisted my plastic fork with an alien hand; I let the rock roll down, down, down and I followed it down. I stood lethargically beneath my own tree. I'd have a long climb to hang a rope here, and need a long rope. I fooled myself about this. There is no true earnestness to existential moments. Now such moments are suffocated by irony and self-awareness. Ever since Nietzsche killed God and Sartre, just repeating Buddha, told us we have an unfulfillable desire for complete fulfillment, our pressing questions and daily actions were most easily answered not with creating authentic meaning and connection to others, but with grounding ourselves in stuff. What better way to combat the poignant inevitability of suffering than to couch it in silk and leather? To surround ourselves with plump sofas, large TVs, and incessant noise? Yes, I oversimplify. Who wants to hear about industrialization, the birth of advertising, and the commodification of the American mind in this setting? Just more digression.

I'd had precursors, existential teasers, when I was a teenager, staring at myself in the mirror and repeating, slowly, "Why are you here?" "Who are you?" "Who *are* you?" I would keep saying this until the room disappeared and my face disappeared and my mind faded and those words and light were the only things. It was enough to feel as if I were going mad. I wasn't. I was coming to terms with something. What they come down to, or add up to, these moments, is the answer to one, deceptively simple question: What do you do with a life? Or a sister question: how can you best be alive in the world? I thought I had answered those. What do you do? You love a woman and you do good work. I'd been doing that for years. Perhaps not bursting with happiness, I was functional and I had moments of pleasure and joy. That's the gamble. You give, and with any luck, you get. Transitory, though. You may go all in, but you always exit with nothing.

Age. Depression. Love. Loss. I should spew this at Ms. Winterson, not talk to you about it, and get the answer once and for all. *Why the fuck is loss the measure of love?* All this agony. All this fuss. Is that age or depression? Same thing. Inevitable declines both.

Other than exchanging money and pleasantries with a pair of bored gas station clerks, I hadn't talked to anyone since leaving Portland. I navigated the limbo of the road, thinking of everything and nothing. Music loud when on. Ocean roar otherwise. Eventually I became lost and needed people to lead me back. I needed someone to see me, hear me, smell me. If no one else is there to witness, do I exist? I saw the girls but they didn't see me. Chameleon, shape shifter, I became who they needed. Does that make me no less real? See me, touch me. I hadn't been touched in eight months, and *I was in a relationship*.

Perhaps inspired by the austerity of the land, I was feeling both bleak and hopeful, still a part of the world in some small way. I promised myself I would get touched. I would have a conversation and flirt and fuck and listen to a woman tell me something about herself, and I would reveal something in return. I would leave pride behind. I was never one to seek pleasure without thought of consequence, but I would make myself into that person for a night or a few nights in order to catapult myself from funk and distraction. What had I persistently advised? *Write it out. Work it out.* I'd fuck it out. That was a form of exercise. Exorcise.

I told myself I would, so I did. I reached San Francisco and sat in a resuscitated Mission Street bar where women sported ink and shots of metal. Worn oak floors and red walls surrounded me. A pool table and small stage with overlarge curtains stood empty. The few patrons wore their requisite black attire and thick-framed glasses, vintage T-shirts and hair tousled at all lengths. Such conformity in their collective push to be individuals. The girl next to me tipped her head. She had K.D. Lang's bipartisan blend, wrinkled shirt and tie, straight jeans over the roundest of hips.

"What's it like to be twenty-one in the gay capital of America?" I asked her.

"I don't know. Fine, I guess. That's a weird question."

"You waiting for someone?"

She shrugged. "Everyone's down at the Elbo."

"Elbo?" Flirting or shrinking, I couldn't be sure.

"Coffee shop bar. There's this spoken word thing twice a month hosted by this big time sex positive lesbian poet that everybody loves."

"But you don't?"

"I don't get the big deal. She strings words together and tells the raunchy story we all live. I guess it's entertaining. The problem for me is this polyamory, sex-rad bullshit. You may get to fuck whoever and whenever you want, but taking someone on a simple date is impossible." She drank her beer.

"You just live in the wrong city."

"And the wrong gender." She emptied her bottle. "I don't mean that." She glanced at me. "What are you doing again? Something about roadwork? You're a truck driver? You don't look like a truck driver."

I'd told her I was on the road, Kerouac style. Spontaneous Kerouac knew flow. Bliss. Knew how to follow it around until it drowned his liver.

"Ever been to Big Sur?" I asked.

"I may be lonely, but I'm not about to go on the road with some old chick I just met."

So I *had* crested into midlife. Crisis justified.

"Kerouac lived in Big Sur for several weeks and Henry Miller for years," I said. "You've got to know Miller. Writer.

Painter. He's the one you read at your age for the sex and at my age for what he says about America."

"You'd probably like the spoken word *her*story crap down the street."

"Although kids now don't read about sex, do they? They find out about it on the internet. Can I get you another beer?"

"No."

"Who turns down a free drink?"

She shrugged.

I sat patiently because the features of flow—skill, challenge, a goal, rules, feedback, concentration, unselfconsciousness, timelessness, intrinsic reward—can all be had in a sexual encounter. The body is a perfect medium for flow, and sex, after all, can be an enjoyable experience. Add a little practice and learned skill, and sex grows beyond enjoyment into something ecstatic. There is an inherent, obvious challenge in sex—to cause, bring about, invite, whatever polite or impolite verb you want to use—orgasm, yours or hers. The rules? Simple. Do things to the other person that cause pleasure. Yes, even if pain is, for that person, pleasurable. Feedback? Obvious. Moans and groans. Movement toward or away. Wetness. Orgasm again. Requests for more. Unselfconsciousness? Sure, just focus on her rhythms and wants. Focus. Timelessness, check. Intrinsic reward, check. Which isn't to say there aren't secondary gains. I sat with the knowledge that San Francisco bars harbor extremists. Whatever you're into, you'll find. And if you don't know what you're into, keep waiting and it'll find you.

I waited. Eons passed. I'd always felt most alone in bars. Acutely alone. That, and unproductive. Slumping on a stool?

Among the five worst ways to pass time. Studying the lip of a glass, waiting for someone or something to take shape. What tedium.

"'The only ones for me are the mad ones, mad to live, mad to talk, be saved, desirous of everything.' You want another drink?" Who knew a skinny-skirted bartender in tall boots and a rockabilly-fitted flannel would be the shape of things to come? "Kids these days. You can't take it personally. They're lost and they have no libido. Maybe the hormones and the ruined food supply," she said. "Big Sur's beautiful. You're just in time for the monarchs. They roost in the eucalyptus trees in Cooper Grove. They weigh less than an ounce yet they fly thousands of miles for a suitable home."

"You're an ecologist?"

"Just a reader. And don't worry, she's right. You're not missing anything at Elbo. Flash-in-the-pan stuff. Still, we all like to see our lives reflected somewhere, even if it's in a shitty poem read aloud in a dive bar. Stick around here. The naked cellist is here tomorrow with her saw player." She topped off my whiskey and soda. "She's fabulous. Wears these knee-high leather boots and nothing else. Tucks the cello between her legs. It's so hot, and she can play. What *does* Miller say about America, anyway?"

"That it's a fruit that rotted before ripening. A black curse on the world."

"Are you going to tell me I shouldn't be here, in the Mission? That I've driven out the Latino population? You're one of *those* women, aren't you? Slum it here for a few drinks, sitting on the stool with your judgment and self-righteousness. Fuck that.

I'm not a black curse. I'm just a girl who wants to run a bar for other girls."

"This is only my second time in San Francisco. I don't know who's gentrifying whom." I turned toward the hybrid girl next to me. "Do I really look that old?"

"Head to Seattle, lady. They have something there called Hot Flash. Might suit you better." She dug into her pocket, tossed a few bills on the bar, and left.

The barmaid laughed. "It's all relative, isn't it? When I was twenty, I was with a forty-year-old. Seemed like nothing for about ten months. Then I realized she was closer to my mother's age than mine. I was so young." She bit her lip, a tad wistful, a tad seductive.

"Makes perfect sense to me," I said. "You can get girls to sleep with you. At twenty, sex is no problem, all that confidence and independence."

"Knowingness, excitement, energy."

"The older woman knows who she is and what she wants. That's hot."

"You sound like you're talking from experience," she said, leaning toward me.

"My first, well, second, was nine years older," I said. "Kris with a K. I thought I knew what I wanted. I thought I was so mature, light years beyond my peers. Really I had no idea. But as I got older the women got younger and now things are different on this side of the equation. I don't seem to hold the same allure for younger women."

"That's what you think."

If you want something, sex for example, you have to ask for it. Everyone's a little shy, a little nervous, even though they want some version of what you want. Confidence is a quick seductress in a women's bar. In certain cities she's a downright slut.

"Ever heard of the zipless fuck?" I asked.

"I don't have underwear on, if that's what you mean."

And there it was—the delightful hum of my foci: nipple, nipple, clit. I was alive in the world. The barmaid sauntered to the end of the counter where she paused and waved her hand for me to follow. We slipped into the bathroom where I grabbed a nitrile glove from the box on top of the tampon dispenser. Muscle memory took over in the tight bathroom quarters. I slid my hand under her skirt, up her thigh, and around to her ass. True to her word, no panties, just clear-felled territory and a welcoming ecosystem. Energy poured from her cunt, intense and welcoming. I told myself I would, so I did. I flirted and I fucked. I felt her hands on my tits, her mouth on my mouth. Alive in the world. She bit my ear and opened her legs further. I slipped two fingers in and out and in and then three, and in my head I saw: Alice tucked up, legs akimbo, in the corner of a bathroom stall. We'd never been so brazen. I tumbled back into the present, disheveled, fingers being suctioned in the soft, warm underworld of a stranger in a not-very-tidy toilet cubby. The pleasant murmur I'd felt in my body disappeared as quickly as it had arrived. In its place: a dead stone of self-consciousness.

I took a breath. "Six years ago this would have been great. Six years ago I would have rocked your world."

"Rock me now. I know it's in you." She pushed against me, my fingers still in her.

"We're like teenagers, necking in the school john. I feel ridiculous."

"Experienced teenagers. Don't stop. Keep that happy hand moving."

Her ecstasy and my indifference. Flow could not conquer Alice, not now. Alice. I'd kept her out of my head for several hours during which hope returned. During which I thought of others. During which I talked to someone new. Hope, now vanished. No chance of finding flow in San Francisco. Still, some part of me didn't want to disappoint the skinny-skirted bartender. I moved my arm, though with less precision, less attention.

"You were good-to-go a second ago. What happened? Zipless, no motive, no regrets. You can't leave me blue."

I didn't want to disappoint, but *blue*? I pulled out, flipped the glove inside out over my fingers and tossed it in the trash. "I'm thinking of someone else."

"Who the fuck cares? *I* don't care. I'm the one reaping the rewards. A fuck is a fuck so long as you're fucking. And forget the damn glove. So long as you don't have a finger fungus or car grease on your hand, I don't care!"

So I fucked her, though I didn't want to. Through her impatience. Spitefully. Irritatedly. Distractedly. Through my impatience. Jammed my naked hand around in her pelvis for another five, eight minutes, bored, detached, utterly self-conscious, until she propped herself on the back of the toilet bowl and brought her hand down to assist, fiercely rubbing the bean between her legs until her whole body surged and her pelvic floor kicked me out.

Literally zipless, but not metaphorically. Not in the least because enjoyment is predicated on how you do something, not what you do, with the attention you give it. With the right frame of mind you can enjoy staring at a white wall, whether the paint is dry or not, while waiting for your oncologist's nurse to invite you into the exam room.

"You want another drink?" She smoothed her skirt and re-snapped her shirt. "It's on me," she said, winking.

"Sure," I said. I had nothing else to do, and empty as I felt, I never turn down a free drink. Back at the bar, I brought the glass to my mouth, and smelled the sharp, sour smell of whiskey and a stranger's vagina. The intimate stranger with whom I was now engaged in something like small talk.

"What's with Big Sur?" she asked.

"I've never been there, just read about it. Thought I'd see for myself what the writers gush about."

"Vacation, then?"

"I'm sure it's nothing like it was sixty years ago, but maybe some of that luster's still there."

"You *are* gonna get on me about gentrification." She smiled and topped off my drink. "You want to tell me who you were thinking about? A bartender's like a shrink, just a whole lot cheaper."

I smiled, a little pained. Sure, bartenders listened to people's stories, but they didn't help change the story. They reinforced the glue to people's masks and delusions. They offered unconditional positive regard so long as the person behaved within an acceptable bandwidth—paying the tab, sitting heavily in a stupor. Bartenders had no idea what really went on in people's lives. "No, not really," I said. "She's in my head enough as it is. I don't want her in the room."

"Fair enough. Tell me about something else, then. What do you do for work?"

"Look, I'm not one for pillow talk, such as it is."

"Humor me."

I sighed. "Psychologist."

"What did you come to the bar for? You can just talk to yourself."

"Yeah, funny. I work at a facility in Oregon, helping teenagers sort out their lives before their lives sort them." Tuesday night. The girls who finished their homework had movie privileges. If no one pulled a classic from the library, one of last year's movies, *Mean Girls*, *Million Dollar Baby*, or *The Notebook* was sure to be playing. One of the teachers had tried to institute yoga on Tuesdays, but no one wanted that. The girls, the ones who didn't remain in dead man's pose the whole time, dramatically convulsed on the floor and sighed heavily, disruptively, flopping like dying fish until Jessica finally threw her hands up and stormed out, inasmuch as a peacenik yoga disciple can storm out.

"A bleeding heart."

"In more ways than one," I said, then decided I didn't want to talk anymore. "Do you want to fuck again?" I asked feebly, thinking maybe I'd like a turn propped on the toilet and that perhaps the rockabilly barmaid was skilled enough to shove me outside of myself.

"Better not, my girlfriend will be here any minute. We're open and all that, but it's been flinty lately and we haven't clarified a few things"

Of course. "You made me complicit against my will?"

"It's cool. Really," she said. "Just, you know, you're a girl in the bar. I shouldn't have even said anything. You've got plausible deniability or whatever that's called."

"Wrong is what it's called."

"It was a fine fuck."

"Yeah, for you."

"I would have reciprocated, but you got all misty-emo."

"It's bullshit to do that to someone."

"Seriously, if you want to talk about it, I'll set you up with another drink and a clean ear. No hard feelings. I'm just a San Francisco bar hag. No harm. No foul. You're taking this way too seriously."

"This is a nightmare. I'd ask you to pinch me, but I don't want you to fucking touch me."

"On second thought, maybe you should go."

"I think I'll wait right here and let your girlfriend smell my hand. Let her wonder how many others there have been. How long have you been together? Have you cheated on her the whole time? She just wasn't enough for you any more? Or ever? Boredom set in? She get busy at work or lose a little interest? Don't answer. Fuck this. It doesn't matter. What's in anyone else's head is none of anyone else's business."

I got up and tossed a twenty on the counter.

"The moonlight will be beautiful along the coast. Enjoy."

I exited, muttering fuck-all to myself, thinking I should have washed my hand. Down the street from the bar was a youth center and a park where a gaggle of teens sprawled on benches and picnic tables. One kid picked at the high strings of a

ukulele while the rest smoked and passed an oversized Mc-
Donald's cup around. Tight pants, balloon pants, pants hanging from the upper lip of asses, skate chicks, word-grrl po-
ets, tattooed, pierced, outliers, seekers, searching for identities
to lay claim to and groups to be part of. Sadly the same everywhere. In the middle of the mess of dirty bodies was the
bipartisan girl from the bar. Her presence among street kids
shouldn't have bothered me. She was closer to their age than
mine, closer in maturity to them, but it did.

"You ditched our scintillating conversation to hang out with
street punks?" I asked her.

"You know this cougar, Bae?" her friend asked.

"She was at the bar a minute ago."

"You know bae is Danish for poop?" I asked.

"Oh, she's chasing. You want some, lady? I'll be nice. You
look so sad. I can be nice to you."

"Some what?"

"Some of my no-ho brown love. I'll give it to ya straight."

Short, quick pulls on the straw followed by grimaces indicated more than fountain soda in the cup. I was never so obvious in my rebellion. I used to secret away in the woods with
friends and joints and Boone's and emerge later under-slept
and sober. Teens today are careless, and because of that care-
lessness they miss out on the illicit thrill of sneaking around.

"What the hell is that?" I asked.

"Oh, ladygirl, don't you see? You've entered the TransRevo-
lution. No-ho. You know, no hormones, no knife to cut up the
parts. A girl who likes girls but feels more like a man inside."

"So you're a lesbian."

"So you're a small-minded cunt."

"C'mon, Nik, don't start any fights tonight. I don't want to sit in the back of a squad again," bipartisan Bae said. "I bought you booze. They'll take me in for sure this time."

"A dyke, then," I said, goading, but still irritable, yet a little curious. I'm of the generation where coming out, though not easy, was certainly more simple. I liked women. I didn't want to be a man or pass for a man. Changing sex parts wasn't an option. Identity games are a mind-fuck and it's only going to get more confusing as technology improves. For the current generation the bigger questions are too big or feel resolved so kids create crises to envelope themselves.

"It's all about redefinition," Nik said.

"Self-definition," Bae corrected.

"You're in the sexiest city in America, lady. Don't you know that? Don't you know that means it's all possible, any little thing you desire, any little thing you can think of?"

"Yeah, self-definition. Only I can be who I am," another in the group chimed.

"Be all you can be!" Yet another.

"You're absolutely right," I said. "You *can* be whatever, whoever you want, and *this* is what you came up with? *This* is the best you can do? Hanging out in a park after midnight, trying to pick up women twice your age? Do something! Anything for chrissakes! Get a job! Read a book! Better yourself in some way!" I couldn't stop myself. "I know you've all got more going in your minds than this. You're better than this. Study something. Cure cancer. Fix people's brains so they don't forget their lives. Pick up trash with your time. You seem to have lots of it. I'm sure there are kitchens and homeless shelters all around here. Isn't that author's place nearby? The Valencia

Project? This is it, you know. One shot. Don't blow it. Be great or be gone."

The mess of them, impassive boulders, sipped and passed the soda cup and stared through me. I threw my arms, useless flags, into the air. Exhausted, rage-filled, a little hoarse, I returned to the car, where I sat, a different useless boulder, for some time. Then with the ocean as wingman I moved along the winding highway. I continued in my solitude and pique, driving a little fast, a little too fast, scaring myself on hairpins and steep slopes. I drove. I kept trying to get the bartender out of my head. I kept pushing Alice into the ocean, and beautifully butch Bae, who was trying to find her—or his—body. I tried to knock the kids aside. Always the kids. The girls, grrls, bois, genderfucks, no-hos, teens. And my girls? What were they doing while I was driving to get out of my head? Wondering where I was. Kyle, with the boy's name, the Boy Named Sue, while a bit androgynous, had no confusion about her sexual identity. Thank the trees for that, she had enough other stuff to figure first. That other stuff is big at that age. At any age. Who am I? What am I for? And *what* am I for when my immediate family can't even secure me. My girls. My girls. Northwest girls are nothing like San Francisco girls who are nothing like California girls who are nothing, nothing at all like Midwest girls. Yet. Still. Sadly the same everywhere.

Big Sur. Nature. Search. I tried to be sensitive to sea and sky. I tried to have my eyes and ears open, but I didn't want to see moonlight or butterflies. Big Sur could no longer be my experience. The bartender had tainted the landscape by dropping her tongue in my mouth and wrapping her cheating cunt around my fingers. This is what happens to the mind when the heart has been stomped by the heel of a boot walking away, walking to someone else. The mind loses hold on reasonableness, and the body reacts in ways inappropriate to the circumstance. Oh, I can map the psychic overload and collapse. I can spew theory and predict behavioral outcomes. I can tell you that betrayal violates a social contract. I trusted Alice to always treat me like I was very, very important to her, but she did not do this. This is a betrayal because the social contract dictates that committed mates make their partners feel important. The mate is the only one with whom you do X, Y, and Z. I can tell you that betrayal also leads to an utter sense of helplessness. The victim feels there is no way to fix the situation. Helplessness collapses into a profound, dizzying, paralyzing depression via loss of self. Shock, disappointment, an upended belief system, and the subsequent sift through the rubble to try to identify the crumbling ledge that led to the fall. Reflection twists into self-blame and guilt. I can tell you all of this and more. I can speak of anger and outrage and an underlying sense of worthlessness. And damage. So much damage. First blow, the social contract smashed. Second blow, the victim's ego crushed. I can tell you all of it, but I can't contain the inevitable jealous eruption, no matter the context.

The problem with being betrayed is you're now victim to reactions disproportionate to incidents and reactions inappropriate to settings. You are all id. You, at one time a vocal teen advocate, will scold your throat dry at harmless kids in the street. You, who fully support a woman's right to define herself and her relationships, will be outraged when a stranger uses you for sex. You, once reasonable and self-aware, once someone who thought before speaking, who saw all sides, who had a firm sense of self, will lose yourself entirely. You will not be able to edit your speech. You will not be able to inhibit your flailing arms or searing, distractible, floating mind.

Smell, touch—scratch touch—taste, sound. The book says flow doesn't have to be physical, nor involve others, that there are forms of flow beyond sex. Ones in particular that don't involve other people, because, as the girls taught me, people are reliable disappointments. There are forms of flow that involve other senses. I could have stopped in wine country and swilled some pinot. Stuck my nose in glasses, sluicing my mouth with oaky red blends that exhibit complex layers of purple and black fruits with tantalizing spicy notes and juicy acidity. Or well-balanced and food-friendly, scrumptiously crisp chardonnays that unfurl layers of bright citrus and pear. Drinking and thinking, raising the glass to the light, watching carefully for the legs to dawdle down the concave glass. Quality! I could have leaned my elbow on the wooden bar and ruminated about the sour cherry notes of the Sangiovese grape marrying beautifully with the darker fruit aroma of a Bordeaux. Or worse, I could have entertained a raucous debate with the sommelier about the benefits of cork versus screw.

No thanks. Wine gives me headaches.

I could have fine dined at the fusion establishments, indulging in dishes that arouse the palate. Please. I am no foodie. Food is practical, provides energy for the body's processes, and I'm no aesthete. I have no refined sensitivity to color and texture, and I'm not indifferent to practical matters.

I always have the recycling out the night before collection. I always stop to urinate when I see the warning of fifty miles until the next rest stop, though I did once stare at a Newmann painting until my eyes dried up and just about dropped to the concrete floor. And I did come across a photograph of a woman holding a man without arms, without legs, in a tub of water. Seeing that felt like someone had tripped me from behind and proceeded to kick me, mostly in the stomach, but also a few times in the head. Rare, those experiences. And not exactly exhilarating. Sublime, unsettling, but not exhilarating. Not optimal experience. Art does much for some people and little for a lot of people.

If I were a different person entirely I could sit unmoving on the beach or in the car or in my very own home that's no longer my home and figure out why an orange can or cannot be chopped up and reassembled into the sun. If I were a different person entirely I could play out infinite chess games in my mind. I could listen to classical music from a folio or link baseball statistics of multiple players to optimize runs batted in. I'm not. I don't have a mathematical mind. I can't achieve such concentration. I've never been able to sever myself from reality.

I was restless. I had stopped at the Miller Memorial Library, a tiny hut of a cabin, tucked beneath a canopy of trees. I stumbled around, realizing it wasn't a library, but an organization, a cultural institution. Not for profit, but still. I drove on and soon pulled off Highway 1 into the JFB State Park parking lot. I clomped down the wooden steps and ambled along the too-wide, too-worn path, through the culvert tunnel under the highway. I stopped at the designated vantage points.

I looked north, west. I saw south. Rugged coastline. Long water. Sky. I read the history that said the waterfall used to pour directly into the ocean. A massive fire, landslide, and highway reconstruction in 1983 filled the cove to form a sandy beach. The dilapidated cabin, Waterfall House, further north was built by Lathrop and Helen Brown and was supposed to be preserved as a museum but instead was torn down by the state in 1965. Lathrop was a congressman from New York. In 1944 and further north, he'd built the Tin House from old gas-station sheeting, then finished its interior with a blue-walled living room. Lathrop and his wife spent one loud night there. The house expanded and shrank with temperature changes, bellowing like a ghost, and clinked and pinged and clanged from rain and sticks and small animals. The Lathrops never returned. You pack up your life, carry it across a wide country, and rebuild. You hate or fear the rebuild. You pack it up and move again. Don't like something? Simple, change it.

Eventually, the waterfall. I was there and I had to see the waterfall, the single most popular image of Big Sur, the 80-foot falls seen from the trail, all that happy, Sisyphean water beating incessantly onto the sandy shore. I drove on, feeling sorry for myself, bypassing field and vineyard, moods shifting like the light and tides, bypassing smog and Botox and silicon. Shunting long nails and status and celebrity ambition, I dropped into the next big city.

Not a sister city with a sunnier disposition, San Diego was no better than San Francisco because I was no better. Learn from history or repeat it. I chose to repeat it with a woman who had the well-worn look of someone who'd had too much sex too soon in life. Her generous use of dark eyeliner and the unfortunate, crude tattoo across the small of her back only emphasized her depletion. Sitting in the beige crystals of La Jolla, trying to cultivate my senses to enjoy the howl of the sea as it met shore, trying to enjoy the radiant glow of a polluted sky, all I could feel was the gritty, dry sand on my feet, legs, in my crotch, on my elbows, in my hair, everywhere. A state of annoyance dominated my powers of focus.

"It's overrated is what it is," I said, grumbling to myself as I futilely dusted sand from my elbows. "And cold. It's cold out here."

"It's not so cold, if you keep moving," a woman said. Her bird legs were wrapped in skinny stonewashed jeans and she wore thin canvas shoes and a pink cutoff sweatshirt.

"You weren't a girl scout, were you?"

"Be prepared. Isn't that for the boys?"

"It's the same for both. There's a shower on the other side of the bathrooms over there. You can just rinse off instead of whatever it is you're doing."

"Does it really come off?"

"You get used to it."

For that brief instant I was engaged in conversation. Unself-conscious banter, a little flirtation. There's skill and challenge in that. Like improv, you have to keep the scene going. What was the first rule? Always say yes. But with that awareness, flow interruptus. Flow undone. Yes? No.

"Don't forget your book." She handed me my road bible, the pages of which held the scribble of a madman's marginalia. "Any good?"

I shielded my eyes with the book. "The sun here is oppressive. I'm not kidding. All day sun, bright and manic. I thought it was what I wanted. What I needed. But Jesus, not this much." There I was talking again. For someone who didn't talk, whose job was to listen, I could've been labeled a rambler or the kind of odd person who relates too-intimate details to unsuspecting ears.

"Thank god it's going down then."

I studied her more closely. Thinner than the thin she should be. Her skin wrinkled, aged. Again, an air of sex despite all that contradicted arousal. I imagined her a groupie who'd fucked everyone in the band and a few roadies. This thought made me feel somewhat sad for her left-out self. Yet, she played along with my shade of crazy, which was comforting.

Dusty was a recovering alcoholic, far enough along where she could be in a bar and no longer have to argue herself out of a drink. "If you don't like sun or sand, what are you doing here?" she asked, as she watched me finish a second beer.

"Traveling." An unwritten and arbitrary rule had established itself in my head. I couldn't tell people about my project. "Vacation of sorts."

"I know your type."

"I doubt it."

"Dodger all the way. You keep just about everything to yourself. Years of sitting through AA meetings offers all sorts of insights into the human soul if you're paying attention."

"Soul, really?"

"Not a believer?" she asked.

"Not particularly. Lack of evidence, defiance of natural laws and such."

"Where's the hope in that?"

"The hope is that people will take responsibility instead of relying on the fear of fire to motivate their actions."

"Even that doesn't seem to work," she agreed.

And then what happened? I did it again because somehow, sometime, somewhere along the line sex equated to optimal experience, to flow. What else were geishas or courtesans or odalisques for, if not to make a male flow? Why else was the porn industry so lucrative?

I had another beer, and we kept talking. Dusty kept accounts for several car repair shops and made jewelry on the side. She was a good listener. She didn't interrupt and held her eyes on mine for appropriate jags of time. I felt soothed enough to follow her home.

A mammoth of a dog, flopped like a lump, leered from the doorway. We were naked and in her bed. Dusty inhaled deeply and pulled away. In all my previous experience, the vagina was not something that needed to be treated delicately, not in the least. Pinched tightly, the skin of her face told me otherwise.

"Are you okay? Did I hurt you?"

"I don't care if it hurts. I haven't been touched in years."

Years? I'd been bitching about a few sexless months. At least during that time I still had a warm body furled close. I sat up on my knees away from her. "I only want it to hurt if that's something you're used to, you know, that you're already into. I can play along but I can't be the first."

"Please?"

I looked at her.

"Really, keep going. It's okay. I promise."

I realized I hadn't been catching whiffs of sex, but a more familiar scent: desperation. At a certain age, an unseen shift occurs, and pleasure is no longer simply pleasure. We are no longer young. We become less capable of that ecstatic, psychotic, state. Time, experience, failure wears and warps us. Layers of complication interfere. We overthink. We second guess. I tried again, this time more slowly, with more lube, with just one finger, but was met with vagina dentata. Her muscles spasmed, the ring constricting entry.

"I thought it'd be easier with a woman," she said, bringing her legs together and turning to her side, curling into herself. "I have this condition. Don't worry. It's not contagious. I thought it might be better with a woman, not hurt as much. Guess I was wrong." She didn't move from her bundled position. "Maybe if you did a little oral."

"I don't do that. Not in uncommitted flings," I said.

"That's where you draw the line?"

I nodded, though secretly I was uncertain if in fact I truly had lines.

"I was in a motorcycle wreck," she said. "It killed my second husband and shattered my pelvis. The pelvis is a ring, you know, and rings always break in more than one place I was told. Couldn't walk for four months. Fifty-two and I had to learn to walk all over again. My muscles remain all fucked up. Dysfunctional pelvic floor, they call it. Fucked up and painful, I say. There's twenty-one. Muscles down there. Twenty-one! The shit you learn."

"How long were you married?"

"Does that matter now? Please. Please just go down on me."

One of the tricks to getting through anything is to act as if. Act as if this stranger is not begging you to eat her conditioned pussy. Act as if this is an everyday occurrence. Act normal. Human. As if you're not half-naked in the bedroom apartment conveniently around the block from a ladies bar in Hillcrest. Act as if there isn't a giant bear in the door about to take your foot off if you try to leave its ailing owner. Act as if you've done it, whatever it is, successfully, a hundred, a thousand times before. Act as if flow is solely physical and not this almost act of hedonism. Act as if your experiments aren't failing. Act as if newness and unknowns aren't absent and connection isn't on hiatus. Act as if this isn't emptiness. Or pain.

With no passport, I couldn't go south, so I went east on I-8 from San Diego. After a night of driving through Arizona's desert, I found myself at the edge of Oak Creek, blinded by Sedona's sun, an unbreaking golden ball suspended over the red dirt and mile-high rocks and low, flat roofs. The movie industry, tourists, and people on a path have infiltrated Sedona's once-hidden rancher's paradise. Known as a spiritual powerhouse, the city is bipolar with its massive, dry red-rock formations and its riparian areas of the canyon, with its elitist shopping malls and commerce and its heavy attention to the ephemeral. Incorporated in the late eighties, Sedona is a young city with young people and retirees and a cornucopia of spiritualism, a southwestern Mecca. Crystal healers here, séance specialists there, energy healers here, Tarot readers there, palm readers, phrenologists, aura stokers. Name it, you'll find it. Beads and feathers and necklaces and stones. Trinkets and talismans and turquoise. Turquoise everywhere. An esoteric turbine of a city. A dizzying, spiritual Disneyland. I needed power. I needed something. Yet I laughed and scanned the city with my derisive eyes. Everyone was so open and earnest and filled with The Energy. Tired from driving all night and spent from my California encounters, I darted for the nearest bed and breakfast, a five-bedroom palatial house at the bottom of a one-lane steep, unmaintained road nestled in a flash flood zone. The owner wore a long thin dress-robe, a sort of sarong combined with a thin drape. She walked barefoot. Her sun-soaked face aged her a decade. "The saying goes," she said, greeting me, "God made the Grand Canyon but lives in Sedona. Welcome to God's house. Take your shoes off and follow me." I swallowed my atheistic and rationalist objection to everything and followed, forcing myself into cordiality so as not to get shut out of the inn.

"Your room is the third on the left up those stairs. This is the common room where we hold classes, such as the one tonight. Breakfast is usually served out here." She stepped onto the back patio, which opened on a gorgeous, unobstructed view. "That's Cathedral Rock. God's house indeed. Magical, isn't it? You came on a good day, but then every day is a good day here. You'll definitely want a cup of tea and that seat at sunset. The way the light paints those rocks is sublime." We continued the tour around the side of the house. "Sauna. Hot tub," she said, pointing, "outdoor shower. We're all very casual here about nudity so if it bothers you, don't look." We reentered the house through another door that led into the kitchen.

"What's with all the turquoise?"

"Turquoise means strength and protection. It's a signal of psychic sensitivity and connection to the spirit world."

"Protection from what?"

"From negative energy. It's also a symbol of friendship. This one," she pulled a turquoise amulet from between her breasts and fingered it, "is from Mark Jacobs. He's a good friend. Known him for years and years. You should go see him. He'll give you a discount on an energy cleanse since you're staying here. He loves this place. But he'll also tell you all about the vortexes, since he grew up in the area and knows everything there is to know. He has a shop in Uptown. That's why you're here, right? It's okay. I can tell you're skeptical. Turquoise also brings peace to the home. I think it's working. I inherited this place after my folks were killed in a crash. I needed a lot of peace back then. You could use some yourself. Your energy is," she twisted and shook her hands frenetically, "if you don't mind my saying."

"I'm just tired. Do you mind if I—"

"What do we do here? We meditate. We self-discover. We sit in the vortexes. They're amazing. It's like a week's worth of Zoloft inhaled in twenty minutes. Sedona refuels the body and rejuvenates the soul. You'll see." She smiled, looking at my eyes—eerie in that she wouldn't look away, yet I didn't think she was really looking at me or into my soul, either. More like how a blind person seems to be looking right at you, but doesn't register a thing visually. I tried to win the staring contest, but couldn't keep focused on her round, deadish eyes so I excused myself. "Oh, yes, yes, get settled in the peacock room, explore the town. See you soon," she said, waving grandly.

I didn't go first and speedily to a vortex. I didn't rush to the energy healer's shop. I imagined an energy cleanse as something akin to a colonic. A long tube. Disgusting output.

Neither of which interested me. I went upstairs to the peacock room and promptly fell into a deep sleep on a turquoise
and brown comforter with cock's plumes on the pillowcases. I
don't think I dreamed, I slept so hard. And long. I woke to
bright yellow walls, a large dream-catcher overhead, and loud,
breathy moans of ecstasy coming from somewhere. Then more
moans, deeper, and another, different one. I counted five dis-
tinct throaty moans and at least two giggling ones. I groaned
and covered my head with a peacock pillow. I was in no mood
to stumble into an orgy.

When I finally rousted myself from the room, I found seven
people, lying on the floor on their backs, fully clothed, feet toward the center, in their version of a circle, or a seven-pronged
star. Arms, necks, torsos writhing, twisting, their bodies emit-
ting moans and groans and guttural yawps. An odd orgy.

"You're awake. Serena said not to bother you. Would you
like to join us?" one of them whispered.

"What have you taken?"

"Oh, no, nothing at all, this is natural. We're thinking off.
Yeah, amazing, right? It's all about breath and energy orgasm. Whole body orgasm. I'm Ruble," she whispered over
the husky breaths and yips. "I'm a sex educator and spiritualist.
I lead groups here every week. Serena must have said. She's
over there, but let her be. She's just found her groove."

The owner of the B&B, lay among the others, in her long
sarong, bucking her hips toward the ceiling, almost levitating.
She let out a single howling, interminable OOOOOOOOOO,
and quivered all over, then collapsed back to the floor. She
licked her lips and rolled to her side, staring through me.

"It's a true thing. See for yourself." Ruble looked lovingly over her neophytes. "This all started in the 80s when the AIDS thing blew up and people kept dying. The founder wanted a way for people to orgasm without killing each other. It really opens up our definition of sexuality. Masters and Johnson got into it a little to put some science behind it. Some people call this Neotantrism, but it all means the same thing. Brain sex. Breath sex. You do know that the brain is the most powerful sex organ, don't you?"

"Of course I do," I said. I bit into my lip slowly, but firmly, testing for pain, for consciousness. Blood. The world just kept getting weirder and weirder.

"I can put out a mat for you and lead you through the breathing and focusing. There's no charge. It's part of your stay. We still have time tonight. These things can go for hours."

"Hours?"

She nodded emphatically, her eyebrows lifting, eyes opening, an image straight from *A Clockwork Orange*. "Oh yes. It's quite ecstatic."

Thinking off. Another notch in the bedpost. Another something to add to the long list of somethings an innocent kid from the Midwest had heard and seen and done. I've strayed too long, traveled too far. "I bet it is," I said, walking toward the door. "I bet it is."

"Come back later for the fire dancers!"

Mixed with inner disdain and not a little desperation, I found Mark Jacobs' store, Crystal Vision, in a small, unassuming storefront in the Uptown Mall. Inside, a kaleidoscopic mess of gems and stones, feathers and photographs, paintings and sculptures, sage sticks, chakra sets of frosted crystal bowls, Reiki books, meditation-relaxation-drumsex-faerie-lore CDs, Tarot and Sedona oracle or crystal ally and other card decks, scented candles and incense, and more. Toward the back in the corner lay a giant pillow like a dog's bed. Mark Jacobs invited me to make myself comfortable. He lit several sage sticks and placed three stones in an arc around me.

"Do you mind if I take a look around your world?" he asked.

I stared at him. I was in *his* shop on *his* dog's bed.

"Your spirit world," he clarified. He stood patiently near. Black leather pants, frilly Shakespeare shirt. Hair creeping from his chest. A barefoot Jim Morrison on the beach.

"You have to ask to do that? Can't you just do that and people won't know?"

"It's respectful to ask. I don't want to impose."

"Okay, then, sure, be my guest."

I don't know what I expected, to feel a chill, to see candles flicker, to hear something not quite like the wind, but nothing changed. I sat there while he perused my spirit world. "Anything good?"

He hummed. I waited.

"You have three. That's good. You have a large Japanese man and two women. Not men and women. I use those terms loosely. One masculine and two feminine presences. They are your protectors. They watch after you."

"I have a sumo wrestler in my corner?"

"Something like that."

I tried to imagine nesting in Sedona. I could have energy orgasm orgies with my three spirit guides and run around in shorts under the despotic sun. I could wrestle with my sumo protector and bathe in sandy vortexes.

Mark Jacobs went on to tell me we have three energy systems: auras, chakras, and meridians. Aura is the energy field that surrounds, enters, and moves out from the physical body. It's made of varying types of vibrations, and the human aura has layers of physical, emotional, mental, and spiritual vibrations. All the colors of the rainbow are in auras and the aura changes depending on the emotion an individual is experiencing. The aura is elastic. Happiness expands it. Sadness or anger contracts it. Auras adjust in size based on population density. In traveling from Portland to Sedona, my aura had grown. If not maintained properly, auras can develop holes. Mark thought I may have developed a hole. "The aura is very thin over here." He swirled the air near my left ear.

Chakras, the spinning wheels of electric energy, also have color and connect us to the collective cosmic energy field, but chakras are more grounded in the body than auras because chakras govern our endocrine system, which regulates aging. Chakras absorb chi, prana, and orgone from the atmosphere and send it along energy channels in the body, transforming it as needed. We have seven major and one hundred twenty-two minor chakras.

Mark Jacobs spoke with a slow cadence and a deep voice. Had I not had a long, bottomless nap, I would have fallen asleep listening to him. He told me the meridians are a system of twenty energy channels within us through which all energy moves. Twelve regular channels flow to the major organs of the body. Eight extraordinary channels are storage bays of energy and are not associated with the organs. We access these channels via the four hundred acupuncture or acupressure points on the skin.

Three energy systems, three stones, three spirits in my corner. I wondered about all the threes. Bad things came in threes—celebrity deaths, for instance, and good things, I supposed. The Trinity: father, son, ghost. Creator, redeemer, sustainer. God's three attributes: omniscience, omnipresence, omnipotence. If you believed in God. The Hindus' trio: unfolding, maintaining, concluding. For Buddhists, the Triple Gem: Buddha, Dhamma, Sangha. Dropping from heaven to earth, consider the life phases: childhood, adulthood, dotage. Mother, father, child. Three primary colors from which all other colors are derived. Three keys of music. Past, present, future. Birth, life, death. Animal, vegetable, mineral. Tripods. Triangles. Three-legged dogs. Three Dog Night.

"Serena said my energy was off, but now I don't know which one," I said.

"Our energy systems are alive. They're intelligent and know what they need for maximal health. They send us messages when something is blocked or damaged, but sometimes we don't listen or can't see or don't know. Doctors are trained to look after physical well-being, psychologists after mental well-being. Energy healers look after the energetic well-being. Others have priests or shamans or rabbis. It's not the same. I will enter and clear you, if you like, and then you must visit the vortexes to be replenished."

Energetic intercourse. Visiting an energy healer went against every psychological PhD tenet of my being, but like a loyal, compliant dog, I sat before Mark Jacobs, self-identified and self-appointed healer.

"The vortex is the funnel shape created by the motion of spiraling energy. The whirlwind, tornado, water going down your shower drain. Here they are swirling centers of energy coming from earth itself."

"Electricity?" I asked.

"Not exactly, but scientists have measured residual magnetism. You go to the vortex and the energy will strengthen your inner being. Are you ready?"

"As ever."

I sat as he scrubbed my aura like a scummy shower and broke down negative energy blockages in my chakras with Black Obsidian Spray. I sat as he smudged all my fields with white sage. How simple, I thought. I should ship him up to The Garden. I sat as he handed me one crystal with his left hand, then another with his right and took them away on a wooden tray. I sat with my three guides and my three fields, getting laundered.

"Past lives," he said. "For another twenty dollars, I can scan your history for impedance."

"I think I've got enough going on in this life."

"You will need to visit four vortex sites in a particular order, which I've written down for you. The journey will not be easy. Looking deeply never is. Once you come out the other side, however, you will know peace. Infinite peace. Just be open to the spirit flowing in and through you. Don't hold tightly to any one thought. The inside world, the spirit world, the energetic world, has to be a sanctuary because the outside world will turn mercenary. Take a rock on your way out."

"Which one?"

"The one that chooses you."

Fucking neo-hippie energy enigma. Energy healers were worse than shrinks with their vague statements. I should have gone to a palm reader for fifty dollars less. Maybe I wasn't gullible enough or open enough. Maybe I didn't have any energy or was too corrupted. I didn't feel any different. The city was an asylum, and I its King of Hearts. I grabbed a black stone with a white streak and shoved it into my pocket.

Back in the peacock room after the scrubbing, I stared at a worn teal, not turquoise, and lime green rucksack I'd picked up at a gear shop. The kid there, the clerk, nineteen, maybe twenty, had been helpful, fitting the straps to my hips and resetting the torso height. He tucked his straying long locks behind an ear and asked what I was up to, where I was headed, in a friendly but not intrusive manner, more curious and genuinely excited than the excessive intimacy grocery clerks and coffee baristas in Portland feigned. I told him about Mark's plan and the vision project. "Right on," he said, touching, almost caressing, his chest where a picture of Steve Martin with an arrow through his head was ironed on. "I stayed out for ten days once. I didn't fast or anything, but I took some peyote and shrooms. Went right to the center of myself."

"What'd you find there?"

"Freedom. Absolute freedom," he said, with such innocence and earnestness that I believed him. He dug into a cargo pocket in his pants and handed me a small plastic bag of what looked like thick moldy potato chips. "You'll see," he said.

The teal and green rucksack had two patches sewn into it. An A inside a heart and an eight-pointed star. I'd be guided by an angry heart, an anarchist heart, and chaos. I wondered how many backs had carried the pack, these symbols, how many mountains and where. Had it only seen red rocks and dry desert and the insides of stores and basements? I'd backpacked a handful of times in the Cascades and farther east in the Wallowas, not by choice. I'd run alone for miles, hours, but strap a pack to my back, drop me in the mountains, and I'm lost and irritated. The last time I'd taken to the wilderness, I was somehow coerced into a six-night trip by Alice. Despite the sharp blue sky, warm air, and a few cloud pocks, we trudged along a thin path through a valley with me grumbling aloud the first three miles.

Alice had whined that I never took vacations and that I needed some balance in my life. She didn't accept my protest that I participated in weekends at the coast because I arrived late on Fridays, went running early or disappeared to work on the book. She thought I was gunning for a full-stop psychic meltdown. On the trail she wanted me to look up, look around, but I couldn't, looking outside my radius set me off-balance. The pack was top heavy. Four miles in, we cut left too soon and crossed a ridge into the wrong valley, though we hadn't realized this right away. The landscape all looked the same back there. We set up camp. Access to the water at the small lake was via mucky, soft earth, quicksand-like. I stepped in and lost my leg to the shin. Socks soaked, camp shoes cemented in mud, I was pissed. "Not a vacation!" Alice had wanted the trip to bring us closer, but it only made me angry. I avoided eye contact and said very little.

The next day, another ridge. More blue sky. The right valley. Another lake with better access. The pack a smidge lighter, its weight distributed better. The same the next day. Day four, we woke to billowy gray, angry clouds. We ate our oatmeal, drank our coffee, loaded our gear, and headed up a steep, open-faced switchback into wild wind and rain. The most rain I'd ever seen, falling heavily everywhere, from every direction, no pattern or breaking point. Dropping my center of gravity as low as possible so as not to be blown off the mountain, I nearly had to crawl to the top. I was soaked through. Relentless, hammering rain. I stared daggers into Alice's back, repeating fuck this, fuck this, fuck, fuck, fuck, in my head as we walked. And walked. Blisters covered my feet. My quads burned on the uphill and my toes ached and went numb on the down. My shoulders chafed from the straps, and I developed a headache from the sustained tug on my neck. Alice had said the experience would be character-building and that people learn all sorts of things about themselves on adventures like the one we were on. I mumbled that I had enough character and she responded that eventually we'd laugh about the trip. The hike was supposed to have been a seven-day loop, averaging eight miles a day, but the punishing rain hiked us out twenty-four miles in one protracted, miserable stretch up and over two passes. Well after midnight, we arrived, limping and waterlogged, at the car.

Unskillfully packed, the lime and teal sack held the essentials: a sparse first-aid kit with a yellow tube for snake bites, alcohol pads, bandages, a handful of drugs, two dry meals, iodine tabs, a Nalgene bottle, a crumpled down vest, and a sleeping bag. Among the many things Mark Jacobs had told me, he also told me to forget the tent. "There'll be too much division between you and the air, and the sky is amazing at night. Don't hide from the sky." In addition to sitting the vortices, *vortexes* as the healers call them, Mark Jacobs had recommended I complete a modified vision quest. Vision quests are rites of passage in many Native American cultures, he'd said. A turning point embarked upon in order to find oneself and one's spiritual and life direction. They're usually taken at the juncture between childhood and adulthood, but can be done at any crossroads. I was supposed to go out for three days and two nights with no food, only water. I was supposed to talk to my spirit guides and listen for birdsong. "When you hear birdsong, you'll know you've connected." Connected to what? I thought but didn't ask. I wanted out of his shop's sage-stained air.

The sack brimmed with essentials and my body filled with fear and hesitation. I felt safe, sort of, in the now familiar beige and turquoise walls of the B&B with its floral bedspread and energy tokens everywhere. TV was a fine enough spirit companion, though the inn had none. I could just stay there, in the peacock room, with the peacock as my protector. And the ghostly moans from the first floor. I wouldn't eat. I could put earplugs in and a blindfold on, recline on a few extra layers of down, creating my own deprivation tank. It was the same, wasn't it? I could hallucinate and connect that way. I'd read the studies, watched handsome, young William Hurt regress into primordial matter. The peacock room wasn't safe, though, because in it I was prey to memory, nostalgia, Alice. I'd tried to leave her in Portland, but she was in that damned bed and at breakfast with me. In the memory of the hike as I prepared for my hike, my quest. On the bed as I remembered other beds, our bed. I grabbed the pack and made for the door.

I went northeast to the first of the vortexes up the trail to the saddle between hills and found the twisted, susceptible juniper trees that indicated where the energy spiraled strongest. The Airport Vortex. Strengthens the masculine side. Self-confidence. Take charged-ness. Standing strong against intimidation and manipulation. Taking appropriate risks. Being decisive. Reason without reality distortion. Then southeast to Red Rock/Cathedral Rock, I walked along the creek into feminine energy. Into goodness. Non-interference. Compassion. Patience. Dependability. In the order I was told, drawing my X, I went next to Boynton Canyon and followed the cairns to the knoll. Boynton balances the masculine and feminine, the yang and yin. And finally to Bell Rock with its sandstone, limestone deposits from hundreds of millions of years ago. Bell Rock strengthens all.

I did this, and maybe felt a little hum, a light buzz over the skin. What else was I going to do? But the hum was no Prozac. No Zoloft. No placebo.

From Bell Rock I dropped into the Mund Wilderness Area as the Arizona sun floated toward the horizon, focusing its glow on the east faces of the red rocks. Stunning, shifting hues of orange, purple, rose. The line of light lowered incrementally, but once it hit the dirt floor, the sky went dark, making everything quiet. Buried-alive-quiet with its black line of jagged rocks, scent of sagebrush, bitterroot, and a sharper, sour smell: me. Chilly and damp Portland rarely crested eighty degrees. I didn't sweat there, but I'd been sweating steadily since San Diego. Dried now, the salty damp settled into funk.

The darkness, not fully dark because of stars and moon. Endless sky. The cosmos. I thought of my energy systems.

They didn't feel, I didn't feel, empty or full, scoured or blemished. I was still I, despite everything. Aside from truly drastic measures, there was no scrubbing that away.

A half-mile walk in any direction brought the same slippery ease of getting lost. Best just to sit on one rock and daydream. I wasn't stupid enough to boulder aimlessly or wander off. That was inviting a fall into the Grand Chasm, the Grand Chaos. I wasn't daring enough. I wasn't willing to enter caves or crevasses, risk a flash flood, water beating me against stone or stone pinning me against itself. I wouldn't get my arm caught and have to saw it off with a dull blade like that kid two years ago. But this was Arizona, not Utah. I was safe, wasn't I? I just had to avoid heat stroke and rattlesnakes and losing my mind for good.

And the wind—whirling dust howling through sagebrush, agave, and yucca, through small holes in rocks, slamming dark omens against my face. The desert floor was nothing like the valleys of the northwest mountains. Here, alone, not having eaten, my mind played toward insanity, turning sinister. Which was worse? The dark or the dark barely lit by stars and moon. Horror of darkness, star-lit wobbly shadows danced in and out of the rocks and bushes. Either way my thanatic imagination spilled forth. Fear was not flow. Soon I would have my own picnic at hanging rock, disappearing, another mystery without solution.

I pulled the bag of rotten chips—peyote buttons—from my pocket and swallowed them one by one. Mark Jacobs didn't advocate messing with the spirits in this way. All I could think of was, "Turn on, tune in, drop out." Misunderstood Tim Leary didn't want the counterculture to get stoned and do nothing. He wanted people to hook into their neural systems and be sensitive to the many layers of consciousness and act harmoniously within the world. He wanted us to detach from unconscious commitments, to be self-reliant, singular, and committed. I was committed. I wasn't going half-assed. I wasn't modifying. I ate just about the whole bag of buttons. I drank some water. I waited. I thought of the High Priest of LSD, nearly a decade dead. How is outer space, Mr. Tim? How is the other side? Oh, death, you are not what I want to be thinking about now. Now, just after ingesting a spineless cactus. Let's talk psilocybin instead and its important reduction of anxiety and depression in people with cancer. Or its purported outcomes of sustained personal growth, enabling a sense of the unity and sacredness of all things. I consoled myself with the idea that I was simply another clinical researcher. An N of one. If all went well, we could build a hothouse and grow cacti, trip the girls out of their nasty ways. I laughed at myself and burped acerbic fluid to the back of my throat. The buttons were bitter, but I drank water and kept them down.

Then I waited.

And waited.

Then.

Then there was skinny-throated Kyle, telling me, "Tim's not coming to guide you. It's you and only you. Make a list, bitch. So your girlfriend dumped you, in a manner of speaking. Dumped you without dumping you. That sucks, dude. But all this self-pity? This stupid flow mission? She was worth dropping out for a week? Life doesn't just all of a sudden stop, you know. This is your fantasy-trip, bitch. The thing to do is make a list. Like you tell us. Write it out, paint it out, work it out.

Find something. All that story therapy crap you tell us. You know, talking being cathartic, releasing the bottled-up shit inside. You're always telling us to get it out in some way. You know, when everything feels like too much or when we don't understand something or when we feel out of control. We should get it out. In a *healthy* way. Then find the flow, bitch. We're not supposed to pop pills or cut or drink or smoke or steal or smash cars with bats," she prattled on, "or spray-paint cuss words on walls or anything. Find the better option. Make the good choice. Dude! Take your own medicine!"

"What else?"

She rolled her eyes. "Story."

"Yes?"

"You have to go back to go forward. You have to understand the past in a new way before you can ever start to make a different future. I know this stuff. The fucking power of story and all. You beat it into us. *Tell your story. Retell your story*," she mimed, "keeping telling it, because at some point you'll shift your ideas about what really went down. Like me. I'm a victim of a lot of shit caused by my fucked dad and mom and their fucked lives, but I don't have to always be the victim. I can see some of the shit I did as acting out, necessary things to survive. At the time."

"Be more specific."

"C'mon, dude, you're not supposed to be shrinking me right now. This is your trip. I'm talking about *you* making a list. Help you get some control over all those little black demon feelings swirling inside you. The list will help calm them so you can choke the shit out of them and not feel the pain anymore. Seriously. You want control again, right? That's what you tell us—storytelling gives us ownership again, *autonomy*. Make the list and write about it. You'll get some distance. Some perspective, like you say. Then you'll get some answers. You won't change what happened, but you'll be able to change your emotional attachment and your reactions. You'll change your feelings about it and yourself. And pretty soon you won't be hating yourself or your lady or anything at all. You see what I'm saying, dude? You have to tell your shit. Whatever went down with your lady. But you know what? Make it funny," she went on. "Humor is a great softener and you're funny sometimes. Be funny with yourself and then write a memoir and sell the rights so they make a movie. A chick flick to replace the dick flick! Or in your case I guess you'd call it a clit flick."

Narrative psych 101. She had it down, echoing me verbatim. She understood the jargon, but was still susceptible to fantasy-land, which makes sense: escapism is a far easier mechanism to employ. But I listened and kicked out the names in the sand.

MIGNON

"You are meeting me at a very bad time." Mignon had said in French-infused English after first sex. A third of it in a bathroom stall, another third in the cramped bucket-seat of my Saab, and the final third in her apartment. We'd met in the street outside a club in the warehouse district. I was leaving before it got too crowded. She was just getting her night started. Already loose with drink, she had grabbed my arm, telling me I wasn't allowed to leave yet. On her living room floor, I told her, "Do your worst. It can only get better."

Mignon Girard. Imagine a wistful smile on my face.

As if twenty-nine weren't difficult enough, dealing with the true advent of adulthood, assessing and reassessing one's life—Am I on the right career path? Shouldn't I be looking to buy a house with a white fence? What are these relationships I've been in, where are they leading me? What do I want? What really matters?—Mignon was twenty-nine with both parents recently dead. Orphaned, with no other relatives to speak of except a busy sister who lived in New York City. They talked on the phone once a month, but only because the sister's therapist assigned this.

Mignon's mother had died of colon cancer a mere thirteen months before I had sex with her firstborn in the unisex stall at

Mixology, a hidden bar in Portland's warehouse district. The stubborn French woman of Russian descent hid her pain until it was too late to do anything about the diseased cells. By the time of her first examination, the cancer had torn through eight inches of her colon, ravaged most of her kidneys and stomach, and was rampaging through her lungs toward the grand fortress, her brain. Two weeks after learning her insides were no longer viable and informing her family, everything about her gave in. She dropped into a coma in the hospital. Her husband made the grueling decision to shut the machines off, and thus end her life. And just when Mignon had finally freed of the anger she felt toward her mother, had finally worked the worst of the grief from her system, her father died. He had a stroke on the eighth hole of the public course he knocked around on alone on Mondays when the course was closed. He'd been gone a mere four months when I was intimate with his daughter.

Mignon said she'd hated sitting through his friends' condolences: "Shame, that one. Didn't even get to finish the first nine." "Died doing what he loved." "Probably was having the best game of his life." And those with darker sentiments: "A stroke for a stroke." "One stroke too many." "The wrong stroke for a Monday." Never mind the fact that his body lay in the middle of the dewy fairway until early Tuesday morning when the groundskeeper came scurrying along in his electric cart.

So much for small talk. So much for first dates and slow growing curiosity. So much for hesitant kisses and tentative first caresses. Mignon called me every day for three weeks. For three weeks we saw each other every night. Roses? No. Some nights she was already drunk by the time I met up with her. Some nights she tore my clothes off and left me with bite marks. Exciting, yes, she kept me guessing, and her grief emerging with a French accent devoid of contractions kept me entralled.

"I was thinking about my funeral the other night. Do not worry. I am not planning anything. These are just thoughts passing. You cannot walk around a hospital half your week, this time of year, with the dying of the light and all, and the dying of the bodies all around you, the faces, weary and lined and sagging, and those eyes. You cannot walk around seeing this and not have such thinking. At the service, I do not want anybody to talk. Only silence and singing. Short lyrical songs. I am not sure which ones, but beautiful. I do not know who will be there. I care not. My parents are gone. My sister, maybe, will be there. It might not be so well attended. That would bother others. But this does not bother me. I will not care because I will not be there because I am dead."

We were on the roof of her apartment complex, rolled tightly in a comforter against the icy wind. Her lone, bare left arm was free from the wrap so she could hold her cigarette and blow pensive smoke into the midnight sky.

"What do you want done with your body?" she asked, but didn't let me answer. "I used to think I would give my body to a medical program. They could cut me up and study all my little parts. That seemed the obvious choice when I was a student in Montreal. I am not sure I want that any more. Americans cutting me up? No."

Mignon was born in Lormont, France, near the larger city of Bordeaux. She came from a family of wine makers. Her father was the second son and was always trying to prove himself to his father, but despite his efforts the vineyard would go to Pierre, his brother. Angered by this, he took his inheritance and purchased a winery in California. Mignon was nineteen at the time and thought America was too radical a change, "Nobody knows the French here," so she went to Montreal for school. Eventually, she followed her parents west, but "California was too much sun and too much golf, so I moved to Seattle and now this place. This is such a funny city. Nobody wants to grow up. They want to sleep until noon and play instruments on their computers and drink terrible beer that is like poorly flavored water."

Mignon had a neglected cat who darted past us as we reentered the apartment from the roof. The gray calico with mean silver eyes relegated himself to the linen closet whenever I was around.

"I turn thirty this year," she said, in another post-coital or drunken conversation. "I am almost through the Saturn Return. You do not know this? The planet Saturn goes around the sun slowly, so slowly. But the Saturn Returns is the time and place the planet returns to the orbit it was in when we were born."

"I don't know anything about this because it's crap."

She ignored me and kept talking. "They say it is an alarm clock when this happens. Choices we make in our twenties are not in sync with our true selves. The cuckoo crows, alerting us we are not who we think we are. Along comes pressure and awareness of death and all our fears gurgle up. And we make different choices to become who we are supposed to become."

"So it means change."

"Yes! Big change."

"That happens to people regardless of what Jupiter is doing."

"Saturn. Jupiter is a whole other box of wax."

"Ball. Ball of wax. Can of worms." Usually I delighted in her mangled English idioms, but when I was annoyed with her, I was annoyed by her mismanaged words. Of course, I knew this wasn't the source of the annoyance. I hadn't heard from her in three days. She'd flown to San Francisco for the weekend. For a conference, she'd said.

"Okay, so you do not believe, but just look at me. Am I evidence enough that Saturn is returned in my orbit? I am a bitch to everyone. I am on the edge of something. Clearly."

"I think your parents' recent deaths have much more to do with your edge than anything weird happening in the heavens. You're grieving. Everything you're feeling and thinking and doing is normal."

I didn't particularly like that Mignon was in turmoil, drinking heavily after hard or easy shifts at the hospital, or drinking gingerly but steadily through a queasy stomach, smoking a pack or more each day, driving recklessly, flirting in bars with strangers, but I did like the idea of being the one stable fixture in her life. I liked that I'd be able to take her home to my family, not as replacement for hers, but as a new model. They'd welcome her and love her as well as any family would. I wanted to provide that, to be the source of new goodness after so much early tragedy. When my mind followed this daydream, I went with it, swallowing back bits of guilt, shreds of opportunism. My savior-complex tucked neatly in recesses while I mused on the notion that going home for holidays would be simplified. There'd be no arguing and settling the sticky matter of whose family to visit on what occasion, whose gets the Christmas privilege and whose the Thanksgiving seconds.

Invincible with strength enough for the both of us, I was absurdly filled with fantasies in those days. A year into my first major job, a year into a promising career helping teens not be teens, I was finally settling into adulthood and all that often accompanies it: 401K, home ownership, ironed clothes, monogamy. I was ready for the long haul. Early moments stretching into years. Anniversaries and flowers and vacations. Bathroom habit annoyances, the sounds of another's bowels, her dishes everywhere but the kitchen, her stilettos hidden mines awaiting me in the night. I was ready. And besides, seeing Mignon come toward me that first night, her gait constrained by a short, tight skirt, no matter the back-story, I couldn't not see her again. And again.

She was an emergency room nurse. Anatomy, physiology, physical pathology—perfect complement to my mind, emotion, personality. Maybe Mignon, once through her thicket of grief, would get into research and the two of us could work on projects—physical emotion and hormonal balance in the female teenager; clinical depression and vitamin D levels in high school sophomores; blood chemistry and feelings of self-worth in homeless adolescents.

I kept these future plans to myself. I wouldn't even joke about them. At that time, I didn't have much clout in the relationship.

"How about a movie tonight?"

"Bleh," she'd scoff and finish her cigarette.

"Dinner at the Mediterranean restaurant in southeast?"

"Not interesting."

"Food is not interesting? Speaking of, have you fed the cat?"

"Oh, him," she waved her arm in dismissal. "No."

"There's a Chekhov play in the Pearl District."

"Chekhov takes me down."

"It's not like he was a professional wrestler," I said before emptying the litter box and putting out hard food for the cat. "He was a doctor who cared for his whole family and was a master of mood and character."

Mignon was full of no, but yes could be my only response. Dancing? Yes. Frenzied groping in the car before dashing into the corner store for more cigarettes. Yes. Camp in the rain on her rooftop. Yes. Watch as she lipped cigarette after cigarette and blew smoke out of her kitchen window. Yes. Sex at four a.m. after little sleep and work at eight. Yes. But when I tried to initiate, "Do not touch the button right now. The button is happy."

Amidst this, the crying jags. Her only words for days, "I am an orphan."

Then, "I am an orphan, but I have a sister. You see, though, we are nothing alike, so it is like not having a sister."

"Be patient. You'll grow closer."

A firm stream of smoke hurried from her mouth. She exhaled strongly when unamused or unimpressed with something I'd said.

Then a shift.

"I need to be alone."

"I am working extra hours this week."

"I have a conference in San Francisco."

"No, I don't want to go out tonight."

After the shift, small hints.

"Do you think sex or emotion gets in the way?" she asked on a walk in Forest Park.

"Gets in the way of what?" She was ahead of me on the trail and I could barely hear her.

She didn't respond.

"I like to think emotion leads to sex and sex then to emotion and the two keep rolling out of each other."

We were quiet for the next mile of the walk, and then Mignon backed herself into a tree and took my hand. "Touch me," she said, pushing my fingers inside her. Stimulated by the forest air and illicit feel of getting caught, I did. She cried when she came, and after she came, she slumped between me and the tree. We held her up, tried to shield her, but also tried to help her let it out, let it all go. Impossible because the it, the intangible, undefined bundle of grief, was always there, hidden away or surfacing, but never, never leaving.

Further into the shift, the sex faded and Mignon only wanted me to hold her.

"This is what I love. This," Mignon said in the early morning when we were both lying awake, before the alarm parted us.

"So do I." But I loved it more after more vigorous forms of holding and touching, though I hadn't said that aloud.

Every day I tried to be good, to strive, to move toward individuation, self-actualization, to see the reflection of the sacred in everyone, even the worst offenders at The Garden, and if I couldn't bring myself to see the divine in them, then at least I would try to see the most amount of good and worth possible in the smallest gestures they made. This was during a period of piqued interest in the Dalai Lama. He'd just been in Portland for four days, campaigning for world peace and compassion in action. I tried to be more compassionate and I tried to be good. I tried to do the right thing by Mignon.

Then small, stupid arguments about misheard phrases or mistaken idioms.

"He is a wolf in cheap clothing," she said, talking about a doctor she worked with who was rude to coworkers and short with patients. He'd brushed up against her a little too closely.

"A wolf in *sheep's* clothing. Sheep," I said sternly. "It's a metaphoric way of saying there's a dangerous person pretending to be harmless. But this guy is not pretending. He's all wolf."

"You know my meaning. And his clothes *are* cheap."

Or:

"It's just an arm and a leg. The trip to Vancouver. It does not cost much, just an arm and leg." She had been worried about money, as she'd spent a lot of it over the months, knowing that she'd be getting some from her father's estate. Nothing had been finalized, however, and she hadn't seen a check. She was trying to justify going off with friends.

"You've got that one backwards," I said, correcting her. "An arm and a leg is very expensive. It means a large amount of money, not a little. Almost half a body's worth."

These were not fun, fake, teasing arguments, but arguments about words or small irritations instead of real issues. I picked her apart because I felt insecure, like I was a transition, a placeholder. I couldn't tell her that, however. She would find me weak and leave as a result.

"I feel pressure," Mignon said, later. "It is not coming from you, but me. Inside."

I loved her. Her anger and angst. Her red lips around white sticks, her mouth puckering out perfect OOOs. I loved her frantic energy and her quick care for injured bodies. I loved her perfect and ruined English. I loved her legs in tight skirts and the way her hand moved over the back of my thigh. I loved her thinking out loud about death or the planets. I loved each of these things, but thought I would have to leave her, if only to reduce the potential heartache. It'd be easier to leave her than be left, not easy, but I'd salvage some esteem, reserve some compassion for myself, if I left before Mignon did, which she was bound to. She'd charted her escape that first night: "You are meeting me at a very bad time." That was her cue that she would eventually exit. But she hadn't left. She held at the chalked X. I came close one night to ending it, saying, "At some point this is going to tip."

"What do you mean by this, tip?"

"Tip toward real togetherness or nothing, not this middle thing."

"What is going to make it tip?"

"Any number of things." The reasons crowded my mind, but that was all I could say. All I could verbalize to Mignon, because giving specifics might manifest them sooner.

"You are so quiet, Lee Bauer."

There it began for her, and so early. The direct acknowledgement of where for her I was not right. This was not an unfamiliar conversation. My silence used to drive Hailey crazy.

To Sam, silence meant more was going on than was actually going on. Silence meant I was bored, in Kelly's view. The fact is, silence, mine and silence in general, is not handled well by others. Silence makes people squirmy or angry or insecure.

Coinciding with this recognition, the faltering, half conversations began.

"What if I can't have sex with you again?" she asked.

"Why couldn't you?"

"Because it would become too intense. You know all my secrets. I am too exposed before you."

"That's where true connection is. That's when sex really gets good. Yeah, it probably will be intense. Especially after all this time, all this talking. So it's intense, feel it. You're safe. What else are we here for, if not to move as close as we can to those places we fear the most? We have these bodies. We have these minds, emotions. I say keep pushing them, keep engaging them." I filled the air with psychobabble shoptalk mixed with not a little sex-positive pop-psych. I watched her turn away and blow a long stream of smoke toward the window.

Later:

"What if you grow tired by my French-English?"

"I won't."

"What if I decide I want to try the penis?"

"You won't."

And then from me:

"Let's move to Vermont. Burlington. It's liberal. Like Portland's east coast sister city."

"Cold in Vermont." Mignon said, and I couldn't tell if it was a question or statement.

"I hear it's beautiful."

"Why would I go to Vermont? I am home here."

The idea was a desperate, futile suggestion, a plea, born of my desire to keep her, to keep her from leaving, to possess her. If we moved, she would come to rely on me in new, other ways and discover it would be difficult to live without me. I saw this pretense clearly and yet still persisted.

"It would be an adventure."

"But your job. My job."

"Kids are in trouble everywhere and everywhere people need nurses."

"No."

I kept at it, picking the scab, not allowing the tissue to heal and scar over.

"It's closer to Toronto and Montreal."

She scrunched her face as though she'd eaten something sour. "I am fine here."

At some point, at some level, I knew my manipulations wouldn't work, that Mignon, once feeling more stable, more herself, able to move about in the world, wouldn't be able to be with me anymore. I was a symptom of Mignon's shadow self. If she stayed in the relationship, I would be a constant reminder of the shitty things she had said and done, of all the pain she'd felt. It would all be right in front of her, neatly wrapped in the body of me. There'd be no clean breaking into a new phase, a new sense of self and possibility.

This was Mignon's own hang-up. I didn't care about the dark heart. "It makes you human," I told her. "Whole."

"This cannot work, Lee. I cannot love someone who loves the worst in me."

"I don't love the worst in you. I love *you*. The good that won't come out."

"You have been a saint."

"I haven't, and I hate when you say things like that."

"You will see. You will get self-righteous, as you should. But sometime, you will hold all of this over me."

"That's not true. That's not true at all. Is that why you think I've stood by you all this time? For power? To get something out of it? I don't want to hold you hostage or get anything from you. I stay because I love you. All along I've seen right past the drinking, the shutting down, missing dates. I've seen right to the center of you. I know you're good. That's what I've been waiting for, for you to see your own potential."

I meant every word.

We endured a difficult three weeks of distance and silence. Mignon wanted more and more time to herself. She didn't let me stay the night. She didn't kiss me in the French way. She didn't call in the middle of the workday to plan the evening. She didn't touch me in return. She didn't ramble on about anything. She didn't wait to come in to finish her cigarette.

Then one night, a phone call.

"Can I come to you?"

"Are you staying or visiting?"

"Staying."

A good night. I didn't ask questions. I didn't push. In the morning she said, "This was only supposed to be casual. A fling with a bar girl. A no-expectations thing while I grieved. While I gathered my things. I was not ready. I was not wanting a relationship, but you, you are so good. You are magnificent. You captivated me and saw me, but with much going on, continuing would not be fair. Have I been fair? No. No."

She'd met someone else.

Several weeks back. She wasn't sure about her then. She was now.

I hate that. Someone going off with someone else and not including the person they're having a relationship with in the decision. Not saying months before, "I don't think I'm happy." It's basic courtesy, not to overlap.

Do you know the derivation of Girard, her last name? Strong with spear. I worried for the cat.

Why was this relationship so hard despite its short life? I can say now the difficulty in getting over her had little to do with Mignon and everything to do with me and my unilateral projections. I had a whole life rolled out for us. She would show me France and Montreal. I would show her Ohio. She would stop smoking and we would listen to Serge Gainsbourg. I would learn French and she'd laugh at *my* language fuck-ups. She had a younger sister as I had a younger sister. They both lived in New York, which was the kind of happy coincidence that led to easy reunions and familial closeness and reconnection. She would ease into her orphaned adult self, wiser and more willing to connect. We would drink all kinds of wine and she would instruct me in the varieties of grapes. Her edges would dull as we grew old and retired to a boring French village whose landscape resembled rural Oregon so closely we would sometimes forget which country we were in. I would welcome socialized medicine and traveling by train. The hurt was in the letting go of all of this, of the strongest of imaginations, and of the sex. But that, too, would have died, I suppose. Given that her Saturn Return sex was full of desperation and carpe diem and sucking marrow. The recklessness and disinhibitions would have passed, and the missionary returned. This one, as well as so many others, was hard because this one carried the death of a possibility. As we get older possibility goes gaunt. We have to feed it when we can, as much as we can, plump it up big and fat.

SAM

Small but wiry and muscular, bearded, with the kindest, shyest gray eyes made ever more striking by the contrast with his pitch-dark hair, Samuel Lovin materialized after Mignon. Sam's face stunned onlookers the way faces do when eyebrows are tweezed too austerely. He tweezed his brows and shaved his legs and lasered his back. You couldn't help but look and look. Dolphin-gentle, yet not so playful, he walked slowly and ate slowly. He spoke softly. He didn't whack spiders with shoes and instead carefully transported them outdoors on a plate or sheet of paper. He was a practicing, non-celibate Buddhist and meditated twice daily in twenty-minute increments. He held several private mantras that he mouthed throughout the day. Mignon lived ennui and destruction, Kelly exuded body and materialism. Sam: the life of the aesthete.

Sam came into my life when my family had finally crossed over to the side of understanding and welcome, the side of unconditional love, and with it, the glorious absence of weirdness. Oh, that weirdness! The dinner when Kris first met everyone, my mom nervously asked her questions like she was an alien who would any second peel back her skin to the mechanized component underparts. And my sister Michelle, through her sardonic teenage angst, tried to connect with Kris by referencing Ferron. My dad said, "Nice to meet you," then berated me about, well, me. I deserved his ire at the time. Utterly lost and out of touch with myself, I was such a fuck-up. Then we sat quietly and scraped our plates and chewed our food and tried not to look at each other. With some practice, we grew out of this awkwardness. Dinners became smoother. My dad came to respect me and my mom realized that lesbians are people, too, actual human people. Then I had to go and disrupt the natural flow of my Midwestern, lapsed Catholic family's begrudging acceptance of a lesbian daughter by bringing Jewish Buddhist Samuel Lovin home to Thanksgiving dinner.

I met Sam two months prior to that Thanksgiving at a conference on Jungian anima and animus in the technological age. We were seated next to each other, which taken alone is mere happenstance, but we were at a Jungian conference, and in the Jungian paradigm there are no coincidences. *Everything* means *something*. That's what's so attractive about Jung's thinking. The coincidences—events without causes—become synchronous. While still causally unrelated, the occurrences carry meaning to the persons involved. But to be synchronous, the events must be unlikely to occur together by chance. The same sort of thinking paves paths to fatalism, lays the foundation of cults, and bolsters conspiracy theories. Eight months single and unlaid, I lunged for any contact. Held in San Francisco, the conference shared top billing with the Folsom Street Fair. I had reluctantly turned my back on that spectacle of skin and leather to attend this fully clothed esoteric one. Likewise, on Sam's end, he'd relinquished his reservation to a four-day bliss sutra program at an ashram two hours south of San Francisco. We both lived in Portland and had been on the same flight, he in seat twelve, me in twenty-one. Given all these coincidences, life could not possibly be a series of random events but an expression of a deeper order.

At the conference, sitting with his legs crossed and fussing his hair, Sam said, "I'm very in touch with my feminine side."

"I haven't shaved my legs in a week," I replied.

We smiled at each other, a connection rife with a familiarity that shouldn't exist. Sam's appearance was just casual enough that when looking at him you thought either you or he had forgotten something. We introduced ourselves. Career status, schools attended, prior conferences, patient population. Sam, from Chicago, had landed in the northwest after college, after touring with an indie bluegrass band. He'd played the fiddle all across the south, in Kansas, Utah, even up to Alaska. He'd liked Portland's arts and music scene, and had made his home there, but after realizing art is never enough and can't pay the bills he went to grad school.

"You live alone?" Sam asked, "in Portland?" as we ate our conference-provided boxed lunches on the hotel steps. "I do," I said, watching his gray eyes, and before I knew it I had told him my poorly edited life story. He was easy to talk to, a skillful listener. Minutes later he'd return to a slight detail or phrase and ask more, and I found myself becoming more curious about him. He volunteered once a month at a soup kitchen and liked to take walks. He was thirty-three, and despite his youth, had a face lined with deep exhaustion. I found myself wondering how taut his abdomen was, and just what he might feel like under me. We met later for a glass of wine, and after, as we stood outside, Sam shifted foot to foot, blowing into his hands to keep warm, a boyish gesture I found endearing.

Back in Portland's lingering October summer, Sam took me swimming—he loved water, particularly rivers, where he could contend against currents—and walking. He took Sunday strolls, starting from his Hawthorne apartment, descending a light grade to the bridge. He wandered through downtown into Washington or Forest Park, dropping over the St. John's Bridge into North Portland. He never had a plan or destination, but would just walk. For miles. Like I ran for miles. My miles taking far fewer hours to cover than his. Sam contained factoids of history and architecture and would tell me about sites like the Weiden-Kennedy building. A 1908 chunk of a warehouse only recently made into a box of light and inversion. We went inside and he pointed out how the building seems to collapse on itself, toying with binarisms of interior and exterior, public versus private, mass and spirit.

"Architecture is the ultimate projection of the psyche, but ordered," he said, eyes bright. "The chaos of the initial idea scribbled by a drunk on a napkin, then in sober light comes the meticulous diagrams with measurements and circuitry. So much goes into a building and yet few really see any of it. Take a spiral staircase. It's the epitome of elegance. Like a woman's stockinged legs, a marriage of curves and function and grace."

Sam's phrasing set me thinking of all the legs my hands had spiraled. The two of us sat quietly on the tiered benches in the grand meeting room where rectangles of light created an illusion of infinite space. Sam could hold silence without pressurizing the air. We could be separate together. After some time, we headed east toward The Old Church where Sam explained that Carpentry Gothic architecture was just Gothic architecture in wood not stone. Then we continued downtown and wandered near the brick buildings beneath the bridges.

"My dad laid roof for thirty years," Sam said. "I suppose that's where my interest comes from. He was always pointing out rooflines and how they interact with the sky. *Interact*. Who says that about their environment? On weekends he would do small remodel projects in people's homes. Kitchens, decks, bonus rooms. His cabinetry work was something to see. That man's patience for correcting a broken angle in an old house was infinite. I would help him summers when I was in college. Try to help him. I'm sure it was much easier for him to do the work alone than to teach me a fraction of the intricacies. He rarely drew a diagram. Kept it all in his head. Two points in time: the room now and the room how it's supposed to be. His sense of symmetry seems impossible to me now. He probably should have been a sculptor of some sort."

"Because he had visual appreciation of his world? That doesn't make someone an artist. Just makes him a witness. A good one."

"My mom hated how rough his hands were, but she was so proud when a neighbor would gush about a new bathroom or granddaughter's nursery. He stopped the tinkering as he called it when my mom died. Sold the house and moved into a trailer in northern Wisconsin not too far from Lake Michigan. The man doesn't have a phone and spends his time reading and fishing."

"Sounds like a full life to me."

"He shed everything."

"We all make our choices."

"I won't know for weeks when he dies," he said. "The thing about buildings is they break down. From day one decay starts in. Chipped paint, groaning foundations."

"The capacity to love the fragile is a hallmark of health."

"I hate that Freud was right about some things." Sam took my hand in his soft warm one. "Churches are decadent and ornate. Libraries are serious and austere or squat planes of pragmatism. Houses reflect personality. The same is true for objects. I suppose that's why I like fiddles. They have small, dynamic bodies with fine necks and delicate peg boxes and fronds. Beauty and function in one."

"Functional because beautiful or beautiful because functional?"

"There's no causality. Beauty *and* function."

"But you put beauty first."

"Only because language requires it."

Sam's kiss was slow and breathy. He was all presence, completely absorbed in the event of kissing, which *was* an event for him, as was every little thing from kissing to practicing yoga to evacuating his bowels. "Everything is about attention and intention," he offered as explanation. He was a little too Bly, a little too Thich Hanh. He whispered a barbaric yawp, rescuing masculinity, wrestling dark angels. Sam had no dark heart, pure, plant-based vegan that he was. Erudite and calm. I often wanted to shake him.

My mother was not amused, not about his eventful kiss, his peaceful warrior masculinity, but about his presence. "You could have warned us, Lee. Given us some hint," she said. She, my dad, Michelle, Michelle's latest hipster, Arik, and I were in the claustrophobic kitchen, made so by too many bodies. It was Thanksgiving Day and Mom was cooking, Dad was getting a new beer, and Michelle was half-heartedly helping Mom. Arik and I loitered and generally got in the way. Sam was in the newly refinished basement, meditating. He and I had flown in three hours earlier and he was rattled from the turbulence. "Just think of it like bumps in a road," I'd told him. He glared at me, as much as he could glare, with his kind eyes. Not the most comfortable driver or passenger, let alone cyclist, he walked just about everywhere and wished he could arrange his life fully to that end.

"I did. I told you to set an extra plate, that I was bringing him with."

"You didn't say *him*. I would have caught *him*. You said Sam. Not Samuel, not Sam the man."

"Not Sam, the girly-man," Dad said, trying to mimic Kevin Nealon mimicking Arnold Schwartzenagger.

"Henry, you're enjoying this far too much."

"You're making too big a deal. It's another damn phase. You should be used to these by now."

"A *heterosexual* phase? Oh, please!" She vigorously pounded boiled potatoes into a limp, lumpy mush.

"You used to think the lesbian thing was a phase," Michelle said. "You used to pray that it was. That she'd find some nice man who'd come along and knock her off her feet or knock some sense into her. And, hey, maybe it was one long ten-year phase. Maybe Sam is that nice man you've been praying for."

"You are all terrible. Just terrible," Mom said.

They had ganged up on her, trapped her in her kitchen, and wouldn't relent. I felt bad, yet amused enough to let them carry on.

"That nice effeminate man who can really give it to her," Arik said.

"Will you shut up about the effeminacy already?" I said, irritated. Sam and I had been dating for two full months and had yet to consummate. "We all know you're threatened by it, but get over yourself."

"Oh, yeah, threatened. Real threatened," Arik said. "I bet he's in your room tweezing hair from his face again."

Dad harrumphed, indicating he was done with the conversation, and made his way back to the welcoming contours of the sofa.

"The problem is," Mom said, "everyone knows now and they all ask how you're doing and if I've met the latest girlfriend and what she does and what *she's* like. If *she'll* be coming home the next holiday. It's all very confusing, is what it is. I don't want to have to explain to everyone all over again."

"You bet it is," I said. "Did you ever think this just might be a little hard for me? Going all this time seeing women and now finding myself with a man? That it might actually be something of a struggle for me? Who's doing all this asking anyway?" As far as I knew, my parents worked and came home and worked again and came home. Occasionally they saw a movie and ate out.

"You love pushing my buttons. Ever since that grungy girl with the hair. What was her name?"

"That relationship had nothing to do with your buttons. Nothing. And neither does this one."

"Family. Coworkers. Our bowling buddies," she said, keeping two conversational trains running.

"Hailey. Her name was Hailey."

"Flaunting it for everyone to see."

"We hid it quite well. Or tried. I tried to. That was a messy, confusing time for me."

There was no rational discussion to be had when my mother brought forth anything and everything from her arsenal of grievances.

"Or that Harley woman. God she was awful."

"You only hated her because she fixed Dad's car."

"It was time for a new car!" After I'd finished graduate school and left for Oregon, my dad junked his Escort and purchased a roaring third generation Bronco, manufactured in our very own backyard of sorts: Wayne, Michigan.

"He loves that car."

"Unnaturally."

"I like him," Arik offered by way of interruption. "He's swishy, but he knows football stats."

"He does?" I asked, surprised by this information. Wall-to-wall bookcases overflowing with candles, prayer beads, books, plants, mandalas, and Micky Hart, Enigma, Dead Can Dance, and The The CDs crowded the perimeter of Sam's condo. There was no football to be found.

Arik nodded and arrowed his bottled beer, drawing attention to Sam and Dad in the living room. "Seems Henry's all right with him, too."

"What the hell are they doing?" Michelle asked.

Sam was cradling dad's head, as if praying over it or studying for lice.

"Craniosacral by the looks of it. Maybe Reiki," I said. "It's very relaxing. Sam is a miracle with migraines."

Ads promoting safe sex say that when you go to bed with one person you're bedding all the people they've bedded. Meaning you don't know what sneaky little something could be coursing their intricate, physical being, so better be safe—pull on the gloves, roll on the condom, wash before and after. The ads are deceptive in their simplicity, small fractions of much larger wholes. The entirety of another's sexual history. You are bedding this one person, yes, and with him, the matrix of his memory and habits, his kiss and yours which are both active, protozoan molds of the thousands of kisses that came before, each one contributing to how the next one will transpire. Behind the current behaviors—squeezing the rounded inner portion of the ass near the sits bones, daring a finger around the rim of the anus, biting or scratching or digging into the other's flesh in some permanently altering fashion, barking, whispering dirty things, choking, punching—behind these are the first times, the memories, the fantasies, the realities of the times with others. Sex, as evinced by the body and its movements, is an everlasting palimpsest.

Sam was not a woman, and while I'd been with men, I hadn't been with any for a solid ten years. This little fact didn't matter so much to Sam, but the sheer quantity and layers of experience I'd had did, though not in a typical jealousy-inducing, crazy-making manner. The palimpsest theory was in Sam's head any time he became involved with someone. Even before we'd had sex, before we'd seen each other naked, he explained, "We are not just you and I coming together. We are all the women you've been with and all the ones I've been with, meeting here now in this union of experience."

"How great is that for you? Quadruples your tally in one night. Orgies for us both!"

He smiled painfully, wearing the look of someone sensitive, someone who was only ever kind and earnest, and yet was always met with others' sarcasm or lack of understanding. He said, still grimacing, still pained, "Sex isn't worth it to me if we're not connecting on the metaphysical level."

I shrugged. "Let's connect metaphysically then."

"We'll see."

"*We'll see?*"

"I'm not sure you take me seriously."

"I do. I do take you seriously. About seventy-five percent seriously. Be happy you're getting that. It's a much higher percentage than the one for myself."

"Let's go for a walk," he said.

"Forget it. I'm going for run."

Then there's the issue of touching others in the ways you, yourself want to be touched, which goes far when both parties are women, but finds itself in a double-dead end when the other is a man. I couldn't fuck Sam how I wanted to be fucked. I couldn't lick his clit clockwise or counterclockwise while slipping two fingers in. Sure, I could bite his shoulder and smack his ass and hope he'd reciprocate, but he was far too passive for that. Shy, maybe. Fearful, likely. He was not violent, nor aggressive. Even play-acting for sex, he couldn't bring himself to fake violence.

Also with Sam, I had to consider condoms and pregnancy and a whole new approach to oral sex reared up. "There's so much more to think about here," I'd told Michelle that Thanksgiving. "I don't know how you stand it." The additional complications mixed with embarrassment and not a little internal confusion about carrying desire for men.

"Just relax your face muscles," Michelle had said. "And don't feel like you have to prove anything. They're always grateful for whatever you do."

"What are you talking about?"

"Giving head. Don't feel like you have to conquer it by taking in every last millimeter. Do what you can and use your hand for the rest."

Sam was exceedingly sensitive. The sex we had was slow and sensual, skilled and caring. His orgasms, full body tiny seizures, were foreign to me. In the beginning his speed and care, prolonged foreplay, drove me crazy and into bed with him more and more. Toward the end, the opposite happened. "Sometimes I just want to fuck. Fast and furious. In and out. Get the job done, sir. Once, just once, can we try it?"

"What is it about that sort of sex that you like?" he asked.

"Are you kidding? You're kidding, right? What's not to like?"

"It sounds like you're overwhelmed by the intensity."

"Of all the things, that's what you're hearing from me? Do I need to make it clearer? I want a quick, hard, mindless, breathless fuck. Even women who find strap-on sex too het-centric are willing to give me what I want on occasion."

"It pains me that you always compare me to the women you've been with."

"It pains me that you don't have a vagina."

Two Wednesdays a month Sam played fiddle with a bluegrass quartet at a tiny bar on Mississippi. Guys in flannel with rolled jeans and girls with patched skirts shifted and slapped their thighs, sometimes singing along with the warble. Everyone so earnest in their desire for authentic experience. To get to know Sam, I went to two shows, then didn't go back.

On a night I drank too many glasses of wine, I took hold of Sam's head and told him if he were a woman, this is what I'd do. Then I performed cunnilingus on his mouth, using one of his gums for the clitoris. He lay still and took it. He was not amused.

"I've been understanding and supportive all along, and you treat me with hostility. What have I done besides offend you with my manhood?"

"Oh, get over yourself. You love the fact that you're the guy who broke the lesbian barrier. You have your bragging rights. Tell all your fiddler friends."

"I understand that it may seem strange, the sex we have, but it's powerful and it's okay to be threatened. Safely, of course."

"Let's talk about threatened. You're threatened of losing control. You're threatened of what it might say about you that you lost control and just fucked with abandon because it felt good."

"No," he said. "That sort of sex is mindless and easy. It's much harder to stay present, in the moment, in tune with your partner."

"Mindless might be easy, but it sure as hell is fun. Let's put the fun back in fucking."

He kept looking at me, all the while practicing his diaphragmatic breathing. "You're no Jungian," he said. "Jung was a deeply spiritual and hopeful man. You're too jaded."

"Jung had affairs. His flesh was weak like everyone else's."

Not too long after that, a week perhaps, we were back in bed.

"If you only had a vagina," I said under my breath, more for me than him, but he had heard me.

"I don't think you see me for me. Let's talk this through once and for all."

"Oh, no. No you don't. I don't want to analyze this to death. We are not in a Woody Allen film. I know better. I'd rather jump in the Williamette."

Many nights Sam and I sat near the fireplace, each reading or I read while he toyed with a jigsaw puzzle. I could tell him about my day, the girls, and he'd offer suggestions for group strategy. He listened and generally put his needs aside for others—for me. Also, he cooked Thai food as if he grew up there. But after a year of his undivided attention and his flat chest, I'd had enough.

"I'm not happy about this," Sam said. "I'm not surprised, but I'm not happy."

"You'll find her," I said. "You'll find the hippie woman of your dreams who wants breathy tantric sex and five-hour orgasms and wants to talk about them for hours. She's out there, your rainbow-hearted androgynous and individuated soulmate."

"And yours?"

"I don't believe in soulmates." A simple fact plainly stated. "The idea implies a single complement or fate. Two were not once one and then split by Zeus, forced to spend a life searching for the other half."

Still listening, Sam was no longer looking at me.

"We're not androgynous souls of later religious thought, either," I continued. "Teaspooned parts male and female, divided into separate genders because someone screwed around with the earth? Forcing the gods to tap us with karma and dooming us to seek our other half over several reincarnations? Crazy. All that gloom before reunion."

"Don't forget about Bashert. Yiddish destiny. Divinely chosen soulmate."

I nodded. "Marriages made in heaven. It's a nice story. Makes for great fiction, but the problem is the presumption of God."

"Let's not go there," Sam said.

My point, which I didn't get to make in that conversation because Sam soon asked me to leave, is that love is a choice. Every day an action. An art. As such, everything remains to be learned about it. Jungian at heart but Frommite in action. If I postcarded this to Sam, he would thoughtfully nod assent. Love is a choice, even the act of it for a single night. Falling has nothing to do with it. Falling is unthinking and accidental. Someone who is not paying attention falls. Falls end in broken bones, bruises, head injuries. An abyss. That's what falling in love is.

KELLY

Everything about Kelly was radiant. The Harley and the leather jacket. The boots. Her blond hair trailing behind as she rode. Her arms. She had great arms, strong and well-defined. Her forearms were fashioned from long, ropey muscles that controlled her hands. Damn, those hands! Kelly Kunkler was pure pleasure. She gave it and took it. All senses, no intellect. All the more astonishing because she was smart. Mechanically smart. She could fix any car and assemble a motorcycle in two days. A modern devotee of Dionysus, born with fire in her belly. Boisterous, joyous, she liked nothing more than to laugh and fuck and eat. She'd clean her plate and whatever was left on mine. Our first time out to dinner, she devoured a large shrimp cocktail, a basket of well-buttered bread, and a twelve-ounce T-bone. She chased each course with bourbon. And then at breakfast the next morning, Kelly asked, "Are you going to eat that?"

"What?"

"That orange slice."

"It's the garnish."

"It's edible."

"Who eats the garnish?"

"So you're not going to eat it?"

"Help yourself."

"Thanks," she said, jamming the slice into her mouth, ripping the fruit from the rind. She didn't balk at fat or carb content, didn't count calories or lament that she couldn't have dessert or a second pastry. For as much as she ate, she was not large. I don't know where she put all the food.

I noticed her blue eyes first. Kelly, it seemed, didn't blink and didn't look away. I soon came to wonder what she was seeing, how accurately she was seeing it, whether she was seeing at all.

Kelly. My first woman after seven years with Kris and my first encounter on the west coast. Kelly worked a tollbooth outside of Portland at the Bridge of the Gods, which unites Oregon and Washington with 1,856 feet of steel. I'd been driving too long, zigzagging my way west out of Ohio, across Illinois, through prairie, steppe, grassland, circling the alien-abduction tower in Wyoming, then climbing through the Tetons, the Sawtooths. Despite my car-crimped body, I'd made a detour over the bridge to see the Columbia from the north side.

"Camping? Going for a hike?" she asked, as I handed her my change.

"I'm not really sure."

"There are tons of great places. You know the bridge itself is part of the Pacific Crest Trail? True factoid. This is the lowest point on the trail, elevation-wise." She looked me over, obviously weighing something in her mind then wrote something on a piece of paper. "Here's an address for a party this weekend. Lots of women. You should come. You better come." She winked at me. "Now get going. You're holding up traffic."

I found out later that Kelly was a seventh-year undergrad. "I'm a senior, but just can't seem to finish," she said, which explained a lot about her way of moving in the world—leaving projects, schools, relationships, unfinished. The first day of her abnormal psych class, a class she would drop before midterms, having gotten a job in a garage, she said, "Everyone's abnormal in some way. I don't need a dude in tweed to tell me that."

She reminded me a little of Kris with her long blond hair and confidence and blue eyes. She reminded me of Hailey with her attention to the senses, though Kelly was a much different, less political, less esoteric version of Hailey. No lectures, no tangents. No art history. No poet-speak. Just the occasional appreciation of an old car. "That's a '57 and no rust! Beautiful shape." Or a nerdy analysis of a hog, "The gasket on that Panther's gonna blow any day."

I went to the party.

"Try, Try, Try," they chanted. "Try, Try, Try!"

I stood on the middle step of a wooden staircase, my left hand holding a loose banister. I was amazed and appalled, aroused and repelled. Banshees, I thought. Maenads. They weren't relegated to myth. They existed. In America.

"Zulu! Zulu! Zulu!" broke between the "Trys."

At the center of the room, a pair of mud-caked cleats flew into the air.

"Try, Try, Try!"

"Zulu. Zulu. Zulu."

A redhead started peeling off her clothes. Off with the soiled and stinking jersey. Off with the sweaty coverall sports bra.

The roar grew more deafening with "Sa-ra. Sa-ra! SA-RA!"

Off with her shorts and underpants in one slick motion. Off with the last garments, the disgusting socks. Stripped down to bare skin, the woman was showered in beer. Laughter and more cries. Grinning, giddy women gone mad. Beer and plastic cups everywhere. The swarm closed in. The naked woman was lifted onto the shoulders of two other women.

I slumped onto the step and watched from behind the wooden bars.

"The boot! Shoot the boot!"

A muddy cleat, perhaps the naked woman's, perhaps not, was passed overhead through many hands. The woman on a throne of shoulders cupped the heel of the cleat and held it out for a willing servant to fill with fresh, white-capped beer.

"Shoot it!"

She tipped the heel to her chin and drained the beer, then tossed the cleat over her shoulder and wiped her mouth with the back of her hand. "Bloomers! Where are the pink bloomers?" she called from her perch. A pair of bright pink boxer shorts was handed up to her. She twirled them by the waistband around her index finger. "Will the lady with the most offside offenses please come forth?"

At this beckoning, the crowd parted and a curly-haired brunette slunk forward. She bowed before the throne of skin and removed her shorts and underwear, replacing them with the pink bloomers.

"On your hands and knees, Miss."

The offender dropped to all fours while the naked woman, lowered to her feet, rubbed her hands together, grinning maliciously. She wound up and smacked the offender's plump, pink ass. "Have at her!" the naked woman yelled. "I have to make the rounds!" Her peach skin blended into the horde of jerseys, and dance music flooded the room.

The drink-up had officially begun. Jerseys flew off, exposing midriffs. The party strained a large and aging Victorian on Hodge Avenue, not too far from the private university. I would have mistaken the rumble for a fraternity party, but there were no restless boys anywhere. Just women. Everywhere. Tall, thin, muscular, large women. Shorthaired, shornhaired, longhaired women. Mothers, sisters, friends, dykes, non-dykes. Housewives, students, lawyers, nurses. Women everywhere, digging each other. All types imaginable, rowdiness their glue, along with rugby and beer. Each had a hand clasped around a cup of frothy amber. Some were holding two. The roar in the room approached concert decibels.

"She had to take her clothes off. She scored her first try today. Her first one ever. It's an honor, her doing that," Kelly explained, standing near me on the stairs, one foot on the floor, her other leg bent and open around me, its foot planted on the stair near my thigh. "A try is a touchdown." She put a joint to her lips and struck a match on her zipper. "She made points for her team. Damn good score, if you ask me."

"That stuff will make you stupid," I said, plucking the joint from Kelly's fingers and pulling on it deeply.

"Part of the tradition," she said, ignoring me, "in rugbyland."

"I suppose you've done it?"

She shrugged noncommittally, and was jerked into a tight conga line, where some hands were on hips and others hidden beneath waistbands. A song erupted:

Why was she born so beautiful
Why was she born at all
She's no fucking use to anyone
She's no fucking use at all

She should be publicly pissed on
She should be publicly shot—BANG, BANG!
She should be tied to a urinal
And left there to rot

So, drink, chug-a-lug
Drink, chug-a-lug
Drink, chug-a-lug and piss

She was born so beautiful
She was born so tall
She's a fucking waste to everyone
She's a fucking waste to us all

The line snaked down the stairwell and I was pushed into the handrail, which teetered out and away from the steps. Through the living room, out into the backyard, the conga headed for the flat, tree-lined neighborhoods of north Portland. I wondered if the naked woman, the redhead, was still in the line, and whether she was still naked. I pictured myself in her place, at the mercy of so many others. Then the rail gave way and crashed to the floor. I picked myself up and scrambled outside for fresh air.

Four shiny, silver kegs displayed themselves in a row, gut to gut, on the back deck.

"We never ice them, if that's what you're thinking. The beer goes too fast to bother." This was from a dirty-socked, shoeless woman with a rainbow scarf tied around her head like a mismanaged turban.

"I don't need it cold," I said.

"You don't believe me? Give it a lift. The first three are already kicked."

"I believe you. But I bet the dousing of that woman had more than a little to do with it."

The colorful turban shook back and forth. "You think we'd waste good beer, tossing it into the air like that? Girl, that's Anchor Steam in them kegs. We buy a few cases of the cheap stuff, pour it into cups and line them up on the counter for the Zulu."

"The Zulu was the beer shower?" I asked.

"And the streaking after. They're both part of it."

"Anything else go on here?"

"Honey, aren't you having a good time?"

"Sure I am. I just wonder if I could be having a *better* time."

"Shit. There ain't no better time to be had."

I was sure my face was screwing into confusion. I didn't get it. The beer and the songs. The little bit of nakedness and the soft leaning toward S&M. The party was breezy and young, skimming the surface of desire. The women wanted more. I wanted them to want more, to reveal themselves. I was about to say as much when the naked redhead skipped up onto the deck, sliding by me toward a keg. She grabbed an abandoned cup from the rail and tossed the contents, then filled refilled it with the warm Anchor Steam. She lifted the cup to her face and guzzled, head foam leaving a mustache. She hip-checked Rainbow Turban and lifted her cup toward me, saying, "Get *her* in a bind and we'd break at least four major bones. My guess is both tibia, one ulna, and the fibula. Fibula'd be the worst. Painful bone to break. Maybe a wrist, though. She's got thin wrists." She drank again. "You don't play, do you?" she asked me.

"She's cherry to all this. Didn't even know what a Zulu was."

"Are you cold?" I asked the naked redhead. "You look cold." Her nipples were alert, attentive.

"A little."

"She must be someone's well-kept secret till now," Turban said. "Someone who was afraid to bring her along, but finally went for it. I smell a settled relationship. Trust and all that shit."

I slid out of my sweater and handed it to Nipples, who donned it.

"Thanks. I'm Sara." Sticky with beer, liquor, and who knows what else, her right hand popped out of the sleeve for a shake. "My try was fucking brilliant, wasn't it?"

"Best this season," Turban said. "You slid right by that full-back. You should figure out a little victory dance like they do in the NFL. The fans love it and it makes your enemies snarl."

"I could drop to my knees and tear my jersey off like Brandi Chastain."

"You'd look like an asshole if we lost the game."

"I suppose." Sara turned her pale cheeks toward me and re-filled her cup. Her ass was solid, like a perfect apple.

"No dimples," Turban said to me.

"True," I confirmed.

"Sara, I'll catch you later." Turban winked at me as she shuffled by.

I stood dumbly, gazing at Sara. I couldn't help myself. The sweater only had three buttons and barely kept her nipples from showing.

"Have you been playing long?" I asked.

"It's my first season. I needed something to help me blow off steam. Rugby's perfect for that. You don't really have to practice, and all the matches are on weekends."

"It's quite the spectacle, that's for sure."

"You don't approve?"

"No one here needs my approval."

An older woman passed. "Sweater off, hon. Your Zulu time's not done."

"Shit. There's more," Sara said, not a note of dismay in her tone.

"*Everyone's* got to see your natural Zulu self. Naked 'til midnight, that's the rule."

"Forty minutes," I said.

She slipped out of my sweater and returned it. "Thanks, anyway."

The music in the house grew louder. Drums thumped relentlessly, until a guitar crashed through with a high-pitched, screaming woman's voice, an angry voice screeching over the other instruments. As if driven out by the music, Pink Bloomers came tearing through the doors. She ducked behind Sara and said breathlessly, "Help, please. You're the only one who can take the boxers off. My ass is killing me. I'll be bruised for weeks."

"Drop 'em, let me see."

Pink Bloomers exposed her full moon.

"What do you think?"

Two bare asses in one night. Highly irregular. "It's red all right."

"Should I set her free?"

I shrugged.

"Okay, you're—wait!" Sara's eyes shimmered darkly as she gazed meaningfully at me. "Since this is your first drink-up, you have to be the last."

Pink Bloomers dropped to her knees, presenting her ass to me, as I again, stood dumbly, gazing about. "Please! Please just do it," Bloomers begged. "Get it over with."

I looked at the pink boxers uncertainly. Then set my cup down and glanced at Sara whose face was lit with eagerness. I took a deep breath, wound up, and smacked the plump ass in front of me so hard my hand and forearm stung.

"Owwwwww!" Bloomers yelled, standing up. She dropped the boxers to her ankles and stepped out. "Thanks, love," she said and bussed me on the cheek before disappearing into the cacophony of the house.

Laughter erupted from Sara's mouth. "I'd say you enjoyed that." She squeezed my arm as she passed into the house, leaving me on the deck with the pink bloomers at my feet.

"What's not to enjoy," I muttered to myself as I refilled my cup.

"You've got to tilt the cup, doll. Cuts away all that head," someone said.

My eyes kept gravitating to the spot where I'd watched Sara drink from a dirty shoe, the spot were she was now, still naked, grinding her backside into Kelly's clothed pelvis. Her movements were rhythmic and seductive. She could have been a high-class stripper or a modern dancer the way she moved. Feeling emboldened and anonymous in a new city, I insinuated my body between Sara's and Kelly's. Sara turned and wrapped her arms around my neck, knocking my beer to the floor. She towed me deeper into the mash of dancers, Kelly too. "I don't care if you never set foot near a rugby field or party again, you're not getting out of here untouched." I grinned, allowing myself to be consumed between them and by the hoard. I was not a graceful dancer. Even under better conditions, in less crowded spaces, I'm gangly and my steps don't naturally follow any beat. And no matter the quantity of alcohol, I'm self-conscious and shove my hips side to side and thrust my shoulders forward and back, gestures I try desperately to make others think is dancing. I was careful not to pin anyone's toes beneath my shoe.

"You've never played a sport, have you?" Sara yelled into my ear, absurdly trying to converse in the din.

"No."

"What do you do?" Sara asked.

"For fun or for money?"

"There's a difference?" Sara yelled.

"Psychologist," I said.

Kelly and Sara looked at one another and nodded agreement to an unspoken thought.

"I live nearby," Kelly said, looking back and forth between us.

"Ten minutes," Sara said. "I can't leave for ten more minutes."

In the kitchen, trashed with bottles and bowls and cracking, hardened dips, Sara slithered an arm into the middle of a mess, and shoved everything aside, sending it recklessly into the sink or onto the floor. She hopped onto the counter and crossed her legs at the ankles.

"You just sat in an evening's worth of fungus," I said.

Sara shrugged. "Grab that bottle."

Kelly grabbed a tall bottle of Ouzo and serendipitously found a shot glass, seemingly unused on the windowsill. She poured herself a shot, then another. The third and fourth she handed to Sara and me.

"What's your story?" Sara said, pawing for the bottle. "I know it's not rugby."

I disliked pointed, yet wide open questions like these.

"Med school," Sara said before bolting another shot. "That's my story."

Assiduous doctor by day, wild banshee by night.

"Helping people," Kelly said.

"Everyone's got to justify her existence somehow."

"What about Pink Bloomers?" Sara asked, looking to Kelly. "A fourth? We could caress her spanked, sore, and bruised ass."

"I'm content with three," Kelly said.

"Are you content with three?" Sara said to me.

"Three what?"

Kelly nodded. "She will be."

After the three of us finished the Ouzo, we left the party for another house in north Portland. Kelly rented space in a smallish craftsman. No one was home, but she slipped a DO NOT DISTURB tag over the handle to her room, which may as well have been a sock over the knob in a dorm. Inside, the three of us were alone. Three? Sara dropped the robe she'd stolen from the Victorian, and once again, was naked. Looking at me and taking my hand, she backed into Kelly, pushing her onto the bed. She pulled me close and kissed me with her cleated mouth.

"I don't want to be a third wheel here," I said.

"You're nice," Sara said, her syllables beginning to slur.

"Nice is for new curtains," I said. I was nervous, electrified. I'd always thought one woman was plenty.

"Exacting, aren't you." Kelly said.

"Knock it off or we're not going to have any fun," Sara said, yanking first the shirt from Kelly's body, then her bra, revealing her pale flesh and puckered nipples.

Aroused, Kelly said in a southern drawl, "Yes, ma'am."

Suddenly there were more hands on me than ever before. My first threesome. Too many hands, too many holes, too many tongues. The reality felt so inexpert and unruly. Who's the top? Who gets the attention? Who comes first? Do we all come? What if you like one more than the other? What if she wants three fingers, but even four of yours are too small? Do you use dildos even if you've used them with someone else? A mouthed suck at my neck and another kissed my belly. I shut off my mind. I ran my hands over Sara's supple body. Someone yanked off my shirt while another pulled my pants free of my legs.

"Wait a sec," Sara said. "I have to pee."

"You don't have to go anywhere."

She stared dumbly at Kelly.

"Piss on me."

And then there's that.

"You're drunk," Sara said, laughing. She tried to lift herself from the bed, but Kelly controlled her pelvis like a rugby ball. Sara concentrated for a second and then relaxed.

Kelly smiled broadly. "Girl, you need to drink some water."

Kelly did everything. No suggestions went unheeded. Handcuffed to the radiator? No problem. Blindfolded and surprised? No problem. The ass? Of course. A quick fingering in a movie theatre. Eat me out while driving down the highway. Anything and everything. She would have scared me had she not been so fun and free. Kelly did not leave decisions to others. If she wanted something, she got it. If she wanted to get peed on, she got peed on. She could go from leaning over an engine, her nose to the carburetor, her arms lost in the metal, to sitting in a salon, having her toenails done with the mother of the new girl she was dating. She rejected shame about class and protocol, about not knowing things other people knew. If she lacked information, she asked without fear. Boundaryless, she allowed the world and all its sensory stroking to delight. Kelly's was the *un*examined life worth living. For that, I loved her.

She was my introduction to Portland, to the West. One afternoon, we found a sandy cove somewhere along the Deschutes River north of Bend. We'd floated down the river, dragging cans of beer in a net. All the while, I fought indolence. Eight years of school followed by residency wrings sloth out of a person. Kelly paddled us to the shore, where we built an elaborate sand castle. As I carved out and filled a moat and found a delicate bark for a drawbridge, I twittered with delight. I felt child-like and content, concentrating, building.

Doubtless Kelly has forgotten the afternoon. I recall the heat and sage, the two matching towers, and the dumb happiness I felt until she planted her feet, and crashed purposefully backwards, onto our creation. At once I felt heartbroken and near tears while she flapped her arms and legs, transforming the ruins into a sand-angel. "Nothing lasts," she said, as she carefully lifted herself from the sand.

She was not subtle, nor tactful. "I'm not with Sara, if that's what you're thinking and haven't asked. We get together sometimes. She's good to go whenever she's in town. Though she's met someone and crossed into monogamy, I think. Ah well." Kelly had never crossed into monogamy, or at least not for long. Same with celibacy. Morning, noon, night. She continually needed to be filled, by food, by sex. The dildos she chose were enormous, and she paired them with anal beads and a foreign tongue ever-present in her mouth. Insatiable. She came hard with squirts and soaked the sheets, which we'd change, only to change again hours later. She was exhausting.

My parents adored her.

The grocery. Kelly at my side, Ding Dongs and Debbies in her basket. We ran into Kris with a K. Kris of the factory floor. Kris of the seven-year stretch. Less than two years since I last saw her had passed, but I still carried her as a lasting imprint on my being. The lines around her eyes had multiplied. Upon seeing her, I felt nervous, shy, nauseated, excited, shaky. And still. Standing still. I would have said more had we met alone. I would have hugged her longer, held her, lingered, had we been alone. I wished we were at the time.

"She'll always be the one," Kelly said in the car later. As ensconced as she was in her own body, she was alert to others' moods and vibrations.

"The one what?"

"The one you'll always wonder about. If you want to be with her tonight, you should. You can. You don't need my permission. I don't mind."

"You're serious?"

"Dead."

For Kelly, there was never anything to forgive, just everything to allow. "Jealousy and monogamy aren't part of my genetic make-up. And that lesbian bed-death thing? That shit doesn't exist in my world."

A relationship with Kelly could only work with constant movement, constant stimuli. Whereas I was at home with a book and blanket, Kelly dove into the world. She wasn't the contemplative sort. She preferred her Harley to a hotel or a campsite. Continual consumption of the nonessential and the quickly obsolete. All for what? To combat a growing vacuum within? Anytime I asked why she did something or why she liked something, inevitably the reason was "It feels good" or "I felt like it" or her most common response, "Why ruin a good thing by picking it apart?"

"So you can understand it and appreciate it even more."

"You take something apart, girl, you never get it together again same as it was. I've been taking things apart all my life and putting them together. Engines. Gears. If something's working just fine, it's never the same after you pull it apart."

"It doesn't have to be the same. That's the point."

"You think you're smarter than me, which is cool. You are about a lot of things. You talk so much about people's motives and what they're thinking, but, you know what? It's the *unexperienced* life that isn't worth living. I hope you find what you're looking for in those books." She rode off, her blonde hair trailing behind her. For months, I got postcards from cities across the states, telling of bars and girls and food and weather. Then I got a few cards from Mexico and Belize, Panama. Then nothing. She stopped writing altogether, short as her notes were. I could only hope, though I suspected otherwise, that she kept living.

I didn't feel decimated when Kelly left. No part of me knocked asunder. We were much too different to be each other's other half. Her leaving hurt, nonetheless because I'd entered a new life, and she was the first of the newness. Undemanding and uncomplicated and fun, yet I couldn't make it work with her. I couldn't cut out on a Friday to blaze to Vancouver. I couldn't pick up strays in bars for threes or fours. I couldn't eat like she ate or take fast corners helmet-less on a motorcycle. I understood only later that sometimes people pass through our lives for short spells, others for much longer, and there's nothing we can do to control how long they stay.

After Kelly, I settled into my work and new home. Into Portland. Interludes filtered through. After Kelly, before Sam, after Sam, before Alice. Interludes. Intermissions. Linda, the one who touched, but wouldn't let herself be touched. Jenn, the jock who wouldn't use dildos. Ann, sensual and sexy who couldn't come. Barb, boozing, bruising Barb. An ultra-feminist sex-ed teacher I met at the women's bookstore, eager to teach me things.

"Here, taste this."

"What?"

"Suck my fingers."

"Your fingers were just inside me."

"I know. Taste yourself."

"What? No! I'm not gay for myself."

"Too bad. It's a beautiful thing."

Tender, young, new to the city, I learned about myself from other women. Grew bold through them.

A waifish one who said she liked it rough, but then stopped me four minutes after we'd started. "You slapped my boob," she said, straight-arming me, holding me off.

I studied the woman's chest. "Boob overstates, but whatever." And then I explained, "Tits. You've got tits. Not boobs."

"Fuck that. At least I don't have udders."

"I do not have udders."

Everyone teaches us something, if nothing else than to look at ourselves as animals capable of being milked.

HAILEY

High school Hailey. High school love. If you can call hormones and sticky fingers love. If at that age lust is love, then
yes, Hailey. Polyamorous and the only one in our peer group
who knew what that meant, fifteen-year-old Hailey Berger
streaked her dark hair with metallic dyes and stomped around
in army boots and long skirts. She liked to stand out. My first
and therefore most devastating. Her position in line means
she marked me in ways no one else could.

"You're the one," I said. I'd caught her in the second floor
bathroom, writing on the wall with a permanent marker. An
unknown graffiti artist had been tagging the school.

"You scared the shit out of me."

I tried to make out the words she'd been writing. "What's
that one?"

"None of your business."

"You're writing on the wall. In the bathroom. For all to see."

"It's not done. That's why it's not your business. It's not
your business, *yet*."

"Caught you," I said, then point to her marker-stained fingers. "Red-handed."

"Funny." She finished her slogan: *Time is a figment. A pig-
ment on consciousness.*

"That one isn't very interesting."

"Who asked you, anyway?"

"My favorite so far is the one near the big trophy case: *Art is a veil of unclean thinking*. That one's good. I don't get this one."

"What do you know about it?"

"The other one does something to my head, spins it. Makes me feel dizzy, like a weird math problem. I feel sort of lost." All these words coming from my mouth surprised me. It was rare for me in those days to talk so much.

"Are you stoned? Do you even know what that's a rip-off from? Forget it. Look, are you gonna rat me out?"

"What's in it for me?" I asked, trying at playfulness. She was annoyed with me, but I was intrigued by her.

She handed me a blue marker. "Write something."

"No way. This is your thing."

"You'll see how good it feels."

"Like what?"

"Don't be tiresome."

"Tiresome? What are you, like, eighty?"

"Just try it."

My mind went blank.

"Don't be an ass."

Stupid song titles were the only things to come to mind. I heard Casey Kasem's voice announcing "Money for Nothing," "She Sells Sanctuary," "Walk Like an Egyptian."

"Never mind. Give me the damn marker."

Sin on my skin, I wrote quickly. I had no idea where it came from. The Jesus and Mary Chain? Love and Rockets?

"Not bad. You've got potential. Maybe. Hey, I have an idea. Can you drive? I have my mom's car, but I hate driving. I have some things to do at the mall. I think you'll dig it."

"I haven't hung out at the mall since junior high."

"Perfect. You'll love it all over again."

"I doubt it."

Learner's permit in hand, I drove her to the mall in her mom's car. Hailey wanted to glue figurines on the dash and a stripe of them down the hood over the top, like a mohawk of trinkets she'd said. "You know. Make it an art car. Artists on the west coast do it. You take some regular, familiar object and morph it into art. Paint it. Glue shit to it. Make it stand out. Make it noticeable."

"It's a car. What's the point?"

"Why not? That's the point. Life is boring and cars are ugly. Might as well make them hideous-ugly. Or ridiculous. So absurd you have to smile."

"Seems like a waste of time."

"You have better things to do?"

"A car takes you from point A to B. Not exactly great art."

"There's no such thing. Not since Warhol plastered a bunch of soup can labels on the wall. Not since that French guy put a urinal in his show. Anything can be art. A piss pot. This stupid car. The body. That lamppost."

"This is your mom's car. Why aren't you driving it?"

"I can't drive. Whatever. Fuck my mom. If you're ever going to get anywhere the first thing you have to do is stop thinking about what your parents have to say about anything, or what anybody says about anything. Park over there."

I pulled the car neatly between the white lines. Hailey leaned over the seat, rummaging in her knapsack.

"You're getting mud on the seat."

"Fuck the mud."

"C'mon, there is such a thing as basic human decency."

"It's too bad you're not into body art. The ultimate expression of narcissism," she said, shoving me out the door and tumbling out after. We entered the mall, Hailey strutting ahead. "Okay, so basically just keep quiet and do as I say." Little did I know that that was to become her favorite line. The first stop was the men's restroom near the food court. Hailey uncapped a marker and strolled right in. Emerging, she said, "God, it's awful in there. Check it out."

"It's the men's room."

"Don't be such a prude."

"What if someone comes in?"

"Act as if *he's* in the wrong room."

"Okay, hang on," I took a deep breath and pushed my way through the entrance to be met by urinals, stinky, caked up urinals. What had I expected? I spun on my heel. "Yeah, it is awful."

I followed Hailey into a department store. We lingered in the women's lingerie department for a few minutes before Hailey said, "Quick, the saleslady's over at the register. Take her shirt off. The mannequin's. Unbutton that shitty blouse and get the teddy off her torso. And hurry up. We don't have much time."

"What?"

"Unbutton that shitty blouse and get the teddy off. Quick."

I did as instructed and undressed my first woman. I rushed at first, nearly knocking her over. Then I slowed down, teasing the plastic through the hole almost seductively.

A year younger and alphabetically, Berger to my Bauer, Hailey sat directly in front of me in three of our six classes freshman year. She used to flap the teacher's handouts at me behind her head, never turning around. That we became inseparable for five months sophomore year is still a mystery to me. One minute she was the ridiculous girl with the crazy hair and crazy outfits who sat in front of me in class, speaking out, interrupting, the next minute she was the crazy girl who wrote on school walls and made the mall fun. Finally she was still the girl in front of me in class, and the girl drawing tattoos on store mannequins, but also had become the girl who got naked and crushed her naked body into mine.

How did the relationship begin? Delinquently. Feeling good by being bad was Hailey's way of moving in the world. Small rebellions that felt so huge.

"We should have taped ourselves," Hailey said before sucking a chocolate malt into her mouth. We were seated in the food court. "That's my fucking ticket into art school. But maybe that's too pretentious. Too self-aware. Image just fucks everything these days."

"I still can't believe you scribbled all over that model," I said.

She looked at me. "Scribbled?"

"It's a ticket straight to juvie."

Later I would be that model. Hailey marked me in a thousand different pens and fonts. Later I opened myself to her in just as many ways. I opened into confusion and doubt and pleasures and guilt, all the while seeing, feeling the art within my own body, and that it was beautiful.

Before Hailey, I hadn't been interested in anything. I wasn't a cheerleader. I didn't play sports. I wasn't in any kind of band. I didn't read or care that much about music. I stood back looking, acting, being bored. If there was something I liked, truly enjoyed, I played it cool for fear of terrible, searing disappointment. The goal of my teenage years was to keep my emotions in check. I'd learned early that if I extended some small part of myself, it came back tangled and bruised, irrevocably deformed. Then what was I supposed to do with it? To avoid mangling I mastered the posture of the incurious, at least outwardly.

Hailey couldn't be broken. She wasn't hung up with self-doubt like most teenagers. She was daring and open. She talked, curious about everything, sparked with energy.

I asked her why she wrote on walls, plastic humans, on bathroom walls, wrapped mannequins like mummies. "I put the writing on the wall," she said. "You know that expression, right? The Bible. Book of Daniel. A mysterious hand appears and writes on the wall while one of the kings is eating. That night he's killed. The writing was a warning."

"Of what?"

"For the king to wake up, just like *they* need to wake up."

"Who?"

"God, are you dense sometimes."

She liked the rush of power. Of transgressions. Of large secrets being revealed. "You against the world," she told me. "You, you, you, you. Don't you ever wonder why you're here? What to do with your life?"

"Yeah, but I guess not in the way you do."

"So, how then?"

"Mostly," I hesitated, "in the bathroom looking at the mirror." Then seeing her lean forward, slightly, her face open, interested, I continued, "I stare at myself in the mirror and ask, 'Why are you here?' 'Who are you?' 'Who *are* you?' I keep saying that until my face kinda disappears and my mind disappears, like those words are the only things." I stopped talking and looked at Hailey, waiting, a bit nervous, for her response.

Hailey sat back, melting into the billowy cushions of her parent's basement sofa. "Awesome, that's the stuff."

I grinned sheepishly.

Hailey was always talking and I was always nodding along. "You ever kiss a girl? In seventh grade I used to go out in the woods with these other kids from the neighborhood and play spin-the-bottle. The rule was, no matter who it pointed to, you had to kiss. French kiss for at least thirty seconds. IN FRONT OF EVERYONE. It was really creepy one time when Jimmy Hayden and his brother Mark were there. Jimmy spun and it landed on Mark. And they kissed. They had to. We made them. And then, when Mark spun, it pointed to Jimmy. As if once weren't enough. Neither of them came back after that day. Mark's in juvie now, keeps getting himself into trouble. I think the whole thing really fucked him up. Anyway, there were a couple girls that I kissed a few times. I liked kissing them so much better than kissing boys. Boy breath smells and is thicker. But kissing girls? So great. I always tried to spin so it'd land on Erica. She had full lips and wore tight shirts. Like she liked her body, you know? I never thought too much of my crush. I just knew I liked kissing girls. I still looked at boys. It's only been in the last year or so that I've come to own my identity. Lesbian, you know? Sounds so much better than *dyke*. Lesbian is foreign. Erotic. The word, I mean. Anyway, I'm in good company: Gertrude Stein. Virginia Woolf. Emily Dickinson. Djuna Barnes. Kiss me," she said. "I'll show you what it's like. You've got to stop backing down from the world. This is it, you know. This is your one go-around. Make the best of it. Try everything."

I hated when she lectured me. To shut her up, I kissed her. I lunged forward, the force of my mouth, face, head, body, pushing Hailey on her back to the floor. Kissed her first out of anger, out of impatience. And then this hostility tipped over into something I didn't have a name for at the time: lust. I grabbed her, in all my fear and anger and confusion, I grabbed fistfuls of her hair, wrapped her with my legs, squeezed, pulled, wrestled her near. "I heard it's always the quiet ones," she said and met each move with equal force, her tongue searching, her body reaching.

Fifteen. Body awake. Finally awake. I didn't want Hailey to say another word. I kissed her more and, still clothed, slammed my pelvis between her parted legs, as if fucking her. But it wasn't enough. I shoved my hand down the front of her pants, and feeling warmth, wetness, feeling Hailey's legs open, I moved into her with two, then three fingers. It was all so natural and unthinking.

"What's that quote from? The one about art being the veil of unclean thinking?"

"It's Nietzsche, but not exactly. It's something about making life bearable through the art of unclear thinking. Not unclean.

But I like my version better. Unclean thinking. I should tell you right now before you get too gaga over me—I don't want you weirding out on me and all—I'm polyamorous."

"Is that a disease?"

"It means many loves. I have many loves. I don't date just one person at a time."

"We're dating?"

"You've had your fingers in me. Duh."

"So?"

She shook her head. "AND, I might want to do these things with someone else. Not yet, but I will. The potential's there. I can't be tied down to any one person right now. Not for a long time, if ever. Look, do you know H.D.? Hilda Doolittle? She was a poet. She said that artists throughout their lives need physical relationships, ones that intensify and draw out talent. Relationships. Plural. More than one. There's no great art without great love and lovers. I'm gonna make all kinds of art. So you see where I'm going with this."

I felt her shift closer, and then I felt Hailey's hand squirm down my pants, her fingers, her paint-stained fingers move inside me. That was all I needed. All I wanted right then.

And again three hours later.

And the next day.

So on for five months.

One night at my house in the bathroom Hailey applied green metallic eye shadow that matched the green of the Manic Panic streaks in her hair. I picked up her thick, black plastic-framed eyeglasses from the counter and put them on.

"These are fake."

"Yeah, but they're fucking awesome. They're the exact style Groucho Marx used to wear."

"That communist guy we read about last week in history?"

Hailey stared at me from behind her dark eyeliner. "You've got no cultural sense, do you?"

"So I don't know about Guido. Who cares?"

"Groucho."

I hated when the crazy blue/green/pink-haired girl stared at me with disdain and disbelief, stared down from her tower.

"We're the same age and you don't know half the things I do." Hailey plucked the glasses from my face. "Anyway, I don't want any misunderstandings here. No hurt feelings or any of the bad shit that comes from polyamory. You know, like jealousy. It's very important to be on the same page every step of the way. Are you listening to me?"

"You sound like a self-help book," I said.

Hailey came close and slipped her hand down the front of my jeans. She did this whenever she wanted, like she owned me. I made to pull away, but she held me.

"I don't care if you see other people," I said.

"You're pissed that you don't know things and I rub it in your face. That I know so much more than you."

"Fuck off."

"Admit it and I will."

"Why do you? You know I hate when my sister does it."

"Why don't you stand up for yourself?"

"What are you looking for—a fight?"

"I'm looking for you."

"You're such a weirdo sometimes."

"I'm always going on and on about what I'm going to do. I get excited over the stupidest things and I never hear you say anything. It makes me wonder, is all. Wonder who you are. Wonder what goes on in your head."

"What's it matter, anyway? Nobody knows who anybody is."

For years I saw that conversation as the moment Hailey began to tire of me. And why shouldn't she? She'd been right after all. I didn't get excited about much. All my energy toward life was her energy, borrowed, usurped.

Eventually, the end.

"You have to stop following me."

"I'm worried about you."

"The fuck you are. You're mad and jealous and want our suffocating little relationship to go back to the way it was."

"Hailey, she's twenty-six. It isn't right."

"What are you—my mother? Age is stupid number, a concept like time."

"I love you. Don't you see?"

"Stalking me is *so* not love. It's pathetic. Look, I told you from the start to keep your options open. It's time to move on."

"They are open. I'll see other people if they come along."

"I'm breaking up with you."

"No you're not. That's not what I want."

"You never know what you want. You wanted this, you and me, only because I put the idea in your head. Because I made it okay for you. You only want me now because you can't have me. You want me and I want Stacey. You see the problem, don't you?"

"You can see her and me. That's what you're all about, right? Poly Poly."

"You can't handle it. Look, the two of us have gone as far as our particular mix can go."

"That makes no sense."

"Think about it. It will. You'll see. Anyway, who knows what will happen in the future. We might be together again. We might not. Think of this as a break if you want. We're taking a break. I need a break from you."

"What's so wrong with me?"

"There's nothing *wrong* with you. All right, you know what? Fuck it. You want to know? Do you really want to know what it is?"

I pleaded with my eyes. I would regret that acquiescence, my desperation for years.

"You're always asking me why I'm doing something. Why I dye my hair. Why I write on walls. Why I want to be with lots of people. Why I think this. Why I think that. Why is the sky blue. It drives me crazy! You're a leech, sucking away at me, sucking my excitement. Find some of your own! Find *something* of your own. It doesn't matter what it is so long as it's yours." She took a breath. "It'll be better this way. You'll get to be with someone else. I know you didn't really have sex with that guy Joel or kiss—what was her name? You made them up and that's fine, I don't really care, but now you'll have those experiences. You're free from your fucked-up feelings about me."

Well, no. Years would pass before that happened. First I had to dismiss and understand a number of things:

I was young.

We were both young.

It was an experiment.

She meant nothing.

I was curious.

We were rebelling.

She was mean.

I was hormonal.

She used me.

Later I would feel angry and resolve never to feel small again.

Even later I would revert to the argument of youth. And my shrink would—my shrink. I *am* a shrink and dislike the shorthand, yet I deploy it. The argument of youth, conveniently, quickly, renders disagreeable thoughts or memories inconsequential and frees me to go on thinking the easy thing, to continue through each day with the tidying knowledge that, yep, we were young and that's why none of it mattered. But it wasn't the folly of youth, and it wasn't simply a matter of being young. Youth. Bedrock and rubble of our later lives. I knew this. I know this. I'd been writing on it, thinking about it for a decade, arguing, rearranging its validity ad tedium. I spent five years looking closely, ever so minutely at the experiences of my early childhood. Going over and over just what it meant that I remember the teacher in second grade who ridiculed how I mispronounced words when I read aloud in class. Scrutinizing what it meant when the doctor called me an animal for biting my fingernails or what it really meant to sit on my uncle's lap while he smoked a cigar and plucked hairs from my arm. Now I allow for the possibility that the psyche is part solid stone, part clay. Only later would I admit that I was affected, in-fected, in substantial ways by my involvement with Hailey.

She was loud and neon and I loved that because I didn't take up space at all.

This, or a form of this, is what I love about working with teenagers, especially the ones in trouble, the smart ones in trouble, who feel too much, think too much, drink too much, who don't take shit and see shit everywhere, who are all walls and anger and something great trying to spring free.

ALICE

What was I doing with my life? Saving myself at that age as many times as I could. And yet I had abandoned the girls. Everyone needs a break sometimes, I told myself. Shrug the shoulders and walk away.

Nothing to forgive and everything to allow.

"You forgot someone. *Two* someones."

My apparition had returned. The girl with the boy's name. Kyle. Ten years from now, keep your ears open. She's got some story. Watch out when she connects with it. There'll be lightning.

"I remind you of you."

"I was nothing like you are. I was a belly-up bitch."

Kyle was a talking juniper, her lined wood wiggled and waved and helixed all around me. My stomach burned and surged. The few contents that were inside met air and sand.

The two someones who didn't make the apparitions list, short as it was, serial monogamist that I am: Kris and Alice. Kris, absent because our separation was slow and sad, not a knifing. Our separation was adult, dignified, and I hate to say: rational. "You have to go," she said. "There's a life waiting for you that's not this life." I couldn't argue. I couldn't bring myself to tantrum and throw things at walls. She was right. I wanted and didn't want to go. I was twenty-six, just out of graduate school and only knew Ohio. My rusting Corsica loaded down, I found I-90 with its sun always in front of me. I went, after seven years. Kris always in my head to hash out the day or close it down with pillow talk. My audience. My advisor. My advocate, devil's and not. Kris, whom I would always wonder about.

Then, the list of infamous names. The women on the bathroom wall of my good times. My mind floods: fondness, anger, regret, intimacy, fights, fucks, first kisses, skin, hangovers, hotel rooms, in-laws. Flashbulb memories. That's the final tally, isn't it? Moments hoarded as old photos in a warped box we pull down from time to time to thumb through, wear and caress with soft eyes. I'm generally not a list-maker, not a to-doer. I don't care for Mr. Post-it or Ms. Sleek-and-Lined-Steno. I keep my ideas in my head until it's time to stretch them, long and furious. My dream journals, for example, now require a seventh volume. To think how the volumes grew from a class assignment. First, a small notebook and shorthand. Soon after, obsession, then expansion to mighty volumes. To hell with reflection or analysis. Not a diary, not even a journal, really. Simply a log. A record of my ongoing inner life. Sometimes I read through it. Old, raw dreams. Fragments. When I record a dream, I write down the details and what the dream means to me in that moment. I never revise. The dream is then locked, fixed in amber, disabled from returning. Someday, I used to think, I would interpret and postulate, develop a cohesive theory from what I've saved, but not any longer. My dissertation cured me of thinking.

Too much thinking makes a girl dull. My use of dreams in couples and group therapy involved neither lists nor outlines. Likewise my abandoned project on narrative psychology and the female teenager, which I discarded just the other day. I'd been tearing forward on that project, thinking I'd have a solid draft by the end of the year.

Just as I thought the visions were over and my life could resume, happy and fully explained, just another shrink made whole again by natural pharmocology, vultures circled and the sky swam around me in midnight Monets.

Then there was silence and memories.

There was Alice in her inked skin and late glass of wine.

There was the time between time, in bed in the early morning, half-awake, warm, naked bodies moving into one another.

There was our first meeting in an acupuncture circle. I arranged myself with twelve other pincushions, the patients in lazy chairs, pants rolled to knees, sleeves rolled to elbows, blitzed by needles. *Normally I don't like circle jerks*, Alice had said. *Too much energy escaping and burrowing. But yours is okay. How do I know you? Have I tattooed you? No? Too bad, you've got great skin.*

There was hope and innocence. Restoration and miracle.

There was blindness, seeing the other through the lens of longing.

There was Alice for two nights between Sam and Mignon, after Hailey, after Kelly, after Kris. Alice again after Mignon, after the intermission.

We walked in the woods in the nighttime, daytime, holding hands. We told each other who we were, who we are, who we might be. We fantasized togetherness in our seventies. Alice's long white hair and small, handsome face, radiant from the years, such good, full years spent with me, handsome and old, with a mop of unkempt hair. We talked. *The last thing you want to hear from your tattoo artist is 'Oh, fuck.'* We entered love and exited the world. Entering the warm body of Alice, exiting everything anywhere else. The elsewhere didn't matter.

The intoxication of art. *You have beautiful skin. You should be tattooed everywhere.*

First kisses across tables. Late nights at The Garden. Hardship during courtship. *Will I see you later? No. Having dinner with Melissa. Again? Mmm. Hmm. It's finally at the point where it's really nice to spend time with her. She's not crazy. At least not right now.*

Alice was friends with all of her former lovers. I was friends with none of mine.

Home and darkness, removing clothes, lying in a narrow bed. Touching and breathing, breathiness, breasts. Desire.

A notion: we could love each other well.

Alice driving too fast.

Waking early and moving close. Listening to her breathing. Her nightshirt damp with night-sweat. Wanting to and not wanting to wake her.

The power of Alice's mere presence, a happy distraction from all else. Alice's thin, long light hair, her strong thighs, skinny legs, and mannish hands. Her six-month phase of dreadlocks, the six hours of washing them out.

Death before death.

I get dibs on dying first. What, you think I want to be hanging around alone when I'm 92? I called it first. Cancer runs strong on my side. You might not get your way.

Quietly steered sex. Turtle-slow. Silk.

Alice soaking in the tub. Me coming home, finding her there, waiting, wanting.

Mornings before we'd lived together, I lay in her bed. She got up to make coffee and walk for the paper. My nerves at her return. Me, naked, in the bed, Alice, dropping the *Times*, her clothes. I rose and dressed. Alice returned to me on the sofa, hiding behind a book.

There were shadows coming into the room.

There was love, what I thought was love.

There was possibility. What I thought was possibility.

And trouble.

You feel superior because of your education, your work, I hate it. You're ashamed of me not excelling at something, not doing more.

No. My heart contradicts itself. We moved in together. Life began and ended. Time stopped, floated. Routines governed: morning coffee and paper, nights at the movies, drinks with friends, my writing, my dreams. Alice running, biking, hiking, Alice, all squiggled ink. Living in the realm of the possible selves. So many lifestyles, numberless models of how to be in the world. I could be someone else. Alice too: consider all her shapeshifting: preschool teacher, coffee shop manager, administrative assistant, construction flagger, library clerk, tattooist. Her interests likewise: Shamanic Journeying, energy work, meditation retreats, yoga, drumming. My late nights at The Garden, my early mornings at the desk in the kitchen. My erotic life uncomplicated and unbeautiful. Trips to the coast. A beach house. The tide filling and emptying the bay. Trips south, to the desert, to the canyon. Always a return to the house, where the air flowed, but felt like it didn't.

Memories.

Our beginning. Alice's mouth glistening from a grand and gooey cinnamon bun, the plate smeared and crusted with glaze. *Don't think this is for me. It's for the baby. Baby Buddha.* She rubbed her belly. *Poor Buddha's going to be born with a sweet tooth. One single, rotted-out sweet tooth.* Alice in her inked skin and late glass of wine. As the end which I did not know as the end, approached, I'd find her sitting by the kitchen window, smoking. Psychosis and deceit. Alice away visiting family, on retreat, at meditation, yoga, I noticed emptiness. I felt her absence. My body was hollow, puppet-like, without Alice to animate me. I handed Alice markers, let her draw on my back. I felt swift lines, jagged straight, up my back over my shoulder, down my arm. A quick glance revealed an abstraction. *Furled tight,* Alice said. *Furled closed. But look closer. There are moments of opening where light gets in. Or out.* Small strong gifted open Alice. And my mind, never failing.

The brawl at The Garden. I tried to break it up and I was shoved into a tree. A small concussion. Headaches and spaciness for weeks. *Why don't you quit? Go into private practice. You'd be great. You'd do so well. Especially after working with those awful girls.* But I was protective of those girls. I loved them and wanted to do right by them, something Alice had stopped trying to understand. *You're underpaid and underappreciated as it is. Why don't you settle on a career? Sorry I'm not more like you. Sorry I haven't found my calling.* People drifted in and out of jobs, whole careers, spending hours their lives at desks, in meetings, deadened. I was a rarity. I dreamed I finished a book. Not a tome on teenagers. A novel, a love-story. I presented it to Alice, who opened it and couldn't read what was written. I looked over her shoulder at the pages. Indecipherable, even to me. Did I wish to remain mysterious? To Alice, whom I loved, with whom I felt exposed? Alice unbuttoned her blouse for me, and I pressed my lips to the space between her breasts. I gazed at her, memorizing contour and detail, before I tasted her and she me. Laughter. Quality and quantity. The fallaway. *Not right now. Not in the mood. I'm premenstrual and I feel soupy. I don't know. I just don't want to.* Naysaying, and self-directed to protect the other, who stops asking, who doesn't push. Denies herself. Fools herself into believing desire is superfluous. A settling as of architecture and earth.

I dreamed Alice and I had broken up, then encountered each other after eight months apart. Alice, coupled again, told me tales of unshakeable passion. A dream that left me angry for days.

It's probably just a phase. In ten years we'll look back on this and laugh. These few months without sex will just be a blip in our long life together.

The stories I was telling myself.

The leaves in the park turned and dried and soft light pushed through the open spaces. The air chilled, the ground dampened. Winter. My favorite time of year. A time of jeans and thin sweaters. The sky and trees battle and riot with color. I walked long in the woods that time of year. On just such a walk, Alice unassumingly: *I think maybe we're not suited all that well for each other.* In silence, I waited, wanting to be sure of Alice's meaning. I'd concocted scenarios before, only to be embarrassed at how badly later I was proven wrong. Missteps make me feel fraudulent as a paid expert.

Time apart. Nights alone.

Desire, Alice's desire, for rupture, forfeit cancellation. Silence. And irrepressible words. Are we suited? The wrong question. Ask about excitement and the willingness to investigate differences. *You're stubborn sometimes.* Alice had a habit of slowness, of deliberate speech and action. Often, later, she seemed elsewhere. When she was thinking, her eyes shifted from point to point, pausing on each object without acquiring it. I used to think she was bored, scavenging the room for something to entertain her. But, no. She just took care.

Alice, on the sofa, her hands an accusative pile in her lap. *Making everyone spell it out. No one gets a pass with you. Spell what out? That I'm not excited any more. That I don't want to continue to bump up against you.* Her eyes shifted away. Resignation and waiting. Nights side-by-side on the same bed, the very frame we'd made together. Nights when Alice would slide close and hold me and I would let her, even in love's absence.

Alice asleep beside me, then awake. Alice unmoved by my movements, my turning on the light to read, my shifting, sighing, seething, my inability to rise and act. Hard and lonely to lie awake all night next to the woman I still loved, who no longer loved me, not in ways I wanted, in ways she once had. Infinitely more desolate to step from the warmth of the loveless bed and pace the dark, silent loft. I had learned this before, before, before, when love was still present. I wandered, hearing a homeless woman rattle a shopping cart down the road, wandered through insomnia, reassured that in the next room, awaited a warm bed and a welcoming body.

Alice's face, her soft, light complexion, empty of everything except her weariness. And my face, marked with lines, concentration, worry, thought-filled hours, hardening, the grooves deepening.

Alice, turning away.

Had I seen her?

In the dark, windless hallucinatory night, I shivered away all that I'd denied, avoided, couldn't see. Dark-sky questions geysered into an uncontrollable deluge of memory that sizzled from my mescalined mind. Several nights in blackout. Shards. Sleep. Wake. Sleep. Half-wake. Half-sleep. Hallucinate. Shiver. SHIVER. Vomit. Sleep. Wake. Wake again. Voices. Bright lights. Motors. Wake. Dust spray from four-wheelers.

"Dude, you all right?"

Teenage voices.

"You don't look so good."

"Are you lost?"

"Happens every year. People think they can find God in the desert. Instead they just find a mean desert."

A woman named Hannah put her hands on my head, and all at once my headache was gone. I calmed. She gave me water and dropped me at the trailhead. I climbed atop a large rock and considered my next move. I lay back against the warm slab. Cronus swallowed a rock thinking it his son Zeus. Prometheus, chained to a rock, fed an eagle his liver for eternity. Virgins bound to rocks. Look Medusa in the eye and turn to rock. And Sisyphus. Can't leave him out. But he was happy, wasn't he? Pushing the rock. Once he relinquished everything beyond immediate experience and stopped looking for anything more, he triumphed. That's the message. Our world and our fate is our own. Our lives are purely what we make of them.

What I was sure of were sturdy cacti, blue jays and doves, lizards, stars, snakes.

I was sure of language. Words. History. Possibility. Redux. Return.

After many nights in the wilderness, I wanted a city. One, but no more. New Mexico—blur of rock and desert. Texas can't ever make an outsider feel at home. I could have darted north to Chicago for an extended stay with a friend. Stone, steel, and brick Chicago. Grounded again, made solid by masonry. Toledo tempted me. Familiarity. Snow. I wanted home. Perhaps a coffee with Kris of the factory floor and first everythings. The last news I had of her was a letter from the farm where she was taking care of her parents.

My one long exercise in avoidance traced a circle that I completed older, weathered, beaten, experienced, then filled it with knowing and not knowing.

The reframing. The story. How I remember it. For now. A girl meets a girl. They stay together for awhile, then part.

What's the story I'm telling myself today? No story. Sometimes some people make you crazy. Most times you just make yourself crazy. The end from the start. The End. Capitals. As in death. Whether the long, slow backwards walk or the quick, tragic one of chance. But other ends, too, when she tires of you or all the banality of daily life trips you into dalliance, collapsing whatever small fortress you'd built. I've gone back, forward. Made the list. I sought flow, which slipped through. I sat in the desert with old and new spirits. Time, not a wound-healer but a wound-sealer, has passed. I've told the story. Not cached away the pain for it to erupt in six months or two years. I may not be better because of it, but at least I've shared it. That's a start.

The final tally: a mind sinking under narratives, if you're lucky enough to keep your mind and retain the vastness of love and emotion, the searing heartache and delight, the fucks, the fights, the compensations, all condensed to a few memories, a few anecdotes. Hoarded. Retold. What felt huge at the time feels small now. Appraise now how love and life intertwine with decline and loss. Endless loss.

From Sedona, I returned to Portland. After the ragged west coast and my days in the desert, I wanted nothing more than the relative quiet of the loft. Voices and music blew in from the street. Weeknight Art Walk. Galleries and other businesses displayed new art on their walls, showcasing local talent. Below, the street filled as more people came in to wander door-to-door, showroom to bar to conversation. I imagined Alice down there somewhere, laughing, looking, her arm linked with someone else's. Alice looked forward to every WAW. Previous works got taken down and distributed to patrons or returned to artists. New, as yet unseen work was hung on waiting walls. Outside, twenty- and thirty-somethings tried to make rent, selling beaded bracelets, painted skirts, or bags stitched together from the plastic of lawn chairs. Maybe Alice was down there, close. Maybe she looked up toward the loft and saw that the lights were out and that the balcony door was battened and that she would be unwelcome here. She would feel the pain of exile, of having exiled herself. Or perhaps she didn't look up, didn't think of me at all, didn't care about the darkened loft she'd recently vacated. I banished the last thought from my mind. Impossible, after five years, for her not to think about me. A simple, irrefutable fact, right? With that uncertainty, I sat on the balcony, and just then noticed the early-arriving darkness as sunlight sprayed the street in a dirty yellow mist. Still cold and drizzling, I folded into myself for warmth.

A block down the street, a man peddled a story-high bicycle. From that distance, in that light, he looked handsome, tan or dark-skinned, but as he approached, his skin revealed itself as a shell of grime. I thought of coal miners, whose grit not even lye can tear through. The dark, choking hours underground. The bike was tall and made from four frames welded together. What effort and planning to ascend and ride that bike. How many crashes preceded mastering it? As he passed, he looked toward me, a vacant grin on his face. Next, the approaching drums of the ragtag marching band. Rata-tat, boom, ba-boom! A group of former high school band members in suits and ties marched up the street. Others in leather and jeans and flowing skirts followed, all lifting their instruments, proudly, hoisting high, donning their scraggly beards, their tattoos, their bifocals. The noise wouldn't die until past midnight. I sighed and gazed at the apartment across the street. Its tenant pulled the curtains closed. I never met that neighbor, only glimpsed his crown of gray hair, smart button-down shirts, dry cleaning draped over furniture. Who was this man with the drawn curtains? What was he thinking tonight? Was he married? Missing someone? Did others matter in his life?

If we're all alone, we're alone together. The notion didn't help.

The incessant phone. Again.

"This is Edna Harrington. You've missed work. You know such absence is a lifetime for the girls. Your work is not done. I expect you tomorrow."

Arriving late for group, I stood outside the door, just out of sight. The girls sat in plastic chairs turned in, out, sideways, or flipped backwards and arranged themselves in their jagged version of a circle. They snapped gum and twirled hair and stole irritated looks at the clock. Kyle stared out the window. I imagined her imagining herself in her farmhouse in the foothills of a mountain range, a few acres of land, trails wending deep into valleys, her hours filled with books, projects. A fantasy of relative solitude, which made sense as the individuals who peopled her world were complete disappointments. Before she could take her first steps toward realizing her dream, she had to change the direction of her story. A difficult feat. Her knees jack-hammered and her agitation grew. What to do and what not to do, annoyed by the natter around her, she was spinning away from her memories, wondering, waiting, as always.

She could risk a mark in her file and bolt from the room. To where? She could hide in her bunk or the common room, even at the phone panel. The gym, the cafeteria, the infirmary, the library, classrooms. That room with the puke-sage walls was also available. Every day the same rooms, the same walls, the same faces give or take, one missing, one added. The same stale air and the same sour, horrible stories. Breakfast at seven, lunch at eleven, dinner at five. Group therapy, family therapy, art therapy, individual sessions. Jobs and classes. I had to guard against tired projection. Privileges for good behavior included DVDs, trips outside, ordering in food. But there were so many in-between hours to fill. Dust the shelves. Practice math. Rake leaves from the grounds. Read another slim novel. Listen to bunkmates complain about food and shitty parents and a fucked-up brother and an indifferent boyfriend. Stare at the sky and its few dead stars. Time waits and ticks and passes and demands to be filled by anything other than deep thinking about the self.

Kyle shifted in her seat, now angrily, arms crossed, knees still bouncing. She looked at the faces of the other girls. Bored, round, bony, fat faces. Faces that didn't seem to care that they were here, sitting here. Again. Vic and Lydel and Carmen and C.H. and Anna, all sitting back, cracking gum, sneering, waiting. "What the fuck? How can you all sit there so calmly?" Kyle shot out.

"Do you have to use that word?" Carmen had recently developed a squeamishness to bad language. "She's just late. In with the DOM or something."

DOM, Director of Madness, a warden of sorts.

"Fuck off, Little Ears," Kyle said. "It's been twenty-five minutes. She's never late and she hasn't been here all week."

Usually I leaned against my desk, looking at the girls as they entered, watching them shuffle or strut, sizing them up, and greeted each one by name. I was never not there, not in the eight months that Kyle had been there, and not since forming the group. Another key to success: just showing up. You win half the battles just by doing what other people in their lives didn't.

Kyle's agitation grew as she watched the second hand's slow, painful march around the clock. She didn't get it, she told me once before. There were bells and buzzers for lights on, for lights off, for breakfast, lunch, dinner, for rec time, for visitations, for work detail, for showering, for shitting, for everything. So, why the clocks? They were everywhere, staring with their white faces and dark hands—tick, tick, tick, shivving her eardrums.

"What's your problem?"

"You're my fucking problem," Kyle said, continuing to kick the leg of Carmen's chair. "The way you crack your gum. Just the fucking look of you."

"Would you calm down? Where's the fire? I don't smell smoke." This was C.H., a behemoth of a fifteen-year-old, so sadly overweight the girls called her C.H. for Congestive Heart Failure. Her too-large body provided her an illusion of safety.

"Shut up, wench. This doesn't drive you crazy?"

Thin, wiry Lydel said, "Isn't it obvious how she can just sit there?" She spoke in sharp darts of sound.

"Pick-on-the-fat-girl day, again, huh? Can't you be a little more creative?"

"Every day is pick-on-the-fat-girl day."

"Look around you, Kyle, where're you gonna go?"

"You should be used to it by now."

"There's no getting used to this."

"You disappear, we won't mind."

"You'll be the first to disappear." Kyle eyed Lydel, who, despite her slight build, had pestled larger girls into the infirmary.

"Oh, big talk, bitch. What are you going to do? Call prison-daddy in?"

"Don't you want to know where she is?"

"Who gives a fuck? She walks out that door, she forgets all about us. She's just collecting a pay check."

Generally tight-lipped, Lydel spoke freely when adults were absent. No one knew all of what she had done to end up in a facility. For most of the girls, some combination of drug use, petty theft, and property destruction sufficed. The rumors around Lydel included prostitution and assault.

"Stop kicking my goddamned chair!"

"There she is. There's the girl with the bad mouth."

"Who gives a fuck?"

"How can you say that? She's the one who signs our tickets out of here."

"That's bullshit. All the stuff she tells us about group theory. How this works."

"That's the thing, sweetie pies, she's not one of us. Never has been. You know anything about her life out there? Didn't think so. You never will either. So fucking sit back and enjoy the dead hour."

"Language! Please!"

"Shut up, hypocrite."

Kyle's bloodless knuckles gripped the underside of her plastic chair. For a moment, I thought I was about to witness a beating that Carmen, in all her meekness, with her newfound religion and her pasty hands and pink nails and snapping gum, might not survive.

"Fu-u-u-u-ck!" Kyle screamed.

"What's up your ass, anyway?"

Kyle clamped her jaw.

"I think the new girl is preggers," Vic said. "Either that or she's getting fat."

"Which new girl? Four came in last week."

"You're one to talk," said Vic.

"The redhead who looks like an albino."

"I think Jeff's giving it to the DOM's secretary."

"She's no redhead. That's a dye-job."

"You're hot for him, aren't you? I see the way you watch him."

"I'd do him."

"He's a fag."

"What's it matter?"

"You'd do anyone."

"Not the maintenance man, whatshisname?"

"Bill."

"If he paid you?"

"Gross."

Kyle didn't care about the new girl or whether the art therapy fag was screwing the secretary in admin. She'd told me, "No one talks about anything real when you aren't around."

"Would you take it in the ass? Doggy-style? You don't have to look at him that way. Why not shit on his dick, say, for a hundred bucks?"

Kyle huffed and went to lean against the wall near the window. She couldn't reveal that she looked forward to group. Couldn't reveal how mindless chatter pained her. She scanned past the woods, toward the horizon, the little of it she could see through the window.

I watched over Kyle as I watched the room.

It's troubling to hold two views of people at once. Vacuous faces and gossip, then personal details. Like C.H. and the curling iron. It was no wonder she was in correctional after what she did to those cats. She should probably be drugged into complacency and locked in a bin for the rest of her life.

"Bifurcated!" Vic said, sitting up in her chair, a piston caught in its upward stroke. "I learned that word last week. It means having two branches or peaks. A bifurcated mountain. Or forked. Like that poem about the two roads. You're on one road, and it bifurcates." She'd been reading the dictionary, one entry at a time. She had mistaken the adage "You learn something new every day" as a declarative statement, "You, there! Learn something new! Every day!" She filled her mind with arcane words and odd trivia. When pressed to explain why, she pinched her bottom lip between her fingers, and said, "I don't know. It's fun, I guess." Clear defense mechanism: distraction.

"The roads are choices," Kyle said.

"What are you talking about now?"

Carmen glared at Kyle. "Please don't kick my seat."

"I said get up. I don't want you next to me." Kyle kicked the seat again, before she sat back down.

"You're going to hell, you know that? You'll be sitting at the foot of the devil."

"Are you an idiot? There ain't no devil."

"There is."

"You know what they do to Mormon girls? They marry them off at fourteen and rape them. And that's just the men."

"I'm not Mormon," Carmen said. "Obviously."

"No? What are you?" Lydel accused.

"Does it matter? Just leave me alone."

"Seems to matter to you. Explain it. I mean, c'mon, after all the shit any of us have been through? What kind of God would allow any of it to happen?"

"It's not up to God. It's up to us. I'll pray for you."

"Then why bother at all with God?"

"It's no bother. You could use Him."

Lydel said, "You believe something. I know you do."

"What?"

"Everyone does. You've got to have something to get you through."

"Through what?"

"Through your problems," Lydel said. "Through the day. You hold on to something that helps you survive."

I was surprised to hear this coming from Lydel. Kyle, though, declined the olive branch and couldn't soften into a reasonable conversation.

"My problems are nothing."

"You wouldn't be here if that was true."

"You trying to convert me to your Wiccan bullshit? Make me eat a live goat?"

"What was all that jumping about when you first got here?"

"I'd like to be doing a puzzle hunt," Vic said.

To be a therapist, you have not only to have a high tolerance for otherness, you have to be positively hospitable to it. Teenagers are alien beings. The alienest of them all.

"A puzzle hunt," Vic said, excitedly. "They have them on the east coast. All over, really. You're on a team and you solve puzzles, which lead to hidden coins. Kind of like a treasure hunt or quest for really brainy people."

"*What* are you talking about?" C.H. asked.

Fantastical escapism. Avoidance. Just as the girls were getting themselves somewhere, Vic changed the course.

"That's what we're talking about, right? What we think about. What we'd like to do when we get out. Lydel wants to get into a band like Sleater Kinney. Carmen wants to be a nun or something. This is what I want to do. I want to go to Rhode Island and do a puzzle hunt."

"Fucking Mensa-dork," Lydel said.

"Like that's going to happen," C.H. said.

"I don't want to be a nun," Carmen said. "No way."

Kyle shot forward, glaring at C.H. "Don't do that to her. Don't fucking do that."

"What, bitch? What am I doing?"

"Beating her down. Killing her fucking dream."

"I'm being real."

"Fuck that."

"She gets out of here, she'll be on watch for a year. Under everyone's scrutiny. I'm being real. Besides, it's a shit dream anyway. Goddamn puzzlehunt for the puzzlecunt."

"Don't take that from her, Vic. Don't listen to a goddamn word she's saying."

Kyle didn't like Vic at first. She thought Vic odd, the way she wandered around, mumbling, not talking to anyone but herself. Then Kyle'd heard a few things about her, things that had happened to her, and how some of the girls taunted her about them, how they did this for no reason other than they could. For Kyle, the harassment explained Vic's ratty hair and belly-to-the-sky personality. Explained the mumbling and her tendency to hide herself away with a big book.

"She's found something she likes. Why do you care? You'd do great at a puzzlehunt, V."

"The way you stick up for her, I'd think you got something going."

"What I've got going is none of your business. You and your stupid ass Sleater Kinney. All trebly and screechy."

"Don't start on me," Lydel said. "Carmen, gimme a piece of gum."

All through this Anna had been silent, absently fidgeting with the stone on her necklace, flipping it back and forth between her fingers. A gift from Egan. He'd found the orange stone at Cannon Beach, broke into the shop room at school to use the lapidary tools. "Orange is wholeness," he'd told Anna. "I drilled a hole through wholeness."

Anna looked up and asked, "What if something happened to her?"

"So what if something did?" Lydel said, blowing a bubble. "They'll get someone else to take her place."

"They would," I said, entering the room. "If I didn't return, they'd find a replacement. It might take a couple weeks and a lot of adjustment, but you'd get settled in with someone else. You would all be taken care of. I apologize for my absence. How has the week been so far?"

"Peachy," Carmen said.

"Yeah, just like every other." Lydel.

I waited. Amidst glares and avoidance and silence.

C.H. asked, "Aren't you going to ask us a question or something to get us started?"

Anna, quiet. Kyle, likewise.

I waited.

"This is bullshit. You should've just stayed home." Lydel again.

C.H. said, "Okay, well, so one day you're sitting in a classroom, trying to follow an algebra expression, spacing out. Then kind of getting it. Then the next day you're getting stoned and taking the pants off some guy twice your age. And the day after that you find out the guy is one of your dad's best friends."

I was glad she'd saved this for group, not family session. I was glad not to have another mother's makeup bleeding into the flushed, horrified skin on her cheeks. The sound of the awful thoughts in her daughter's head, her awful deeds in action. Mothers are always shocked, shocked. But still, I waited.

"You sucked off your dad's friend?"

"I didn't know who he was!"

"How can you not know? Why would you do an old dude anyway!"

"My dad wasn't around much."

Pop! went Lydel's gum.

"He comes to group."

"He has to. My mom took off."

"How does that make you feel?" Vic mocked, and they all looked at me.

I waited.

"That's it? You apologize and that's fucking it?" There it was, finally. Kyle couldn't hold back. "You can't disappear and leave us all here. No one said a thing. And don't tell me to say more because I just said it all."

"Shit, she can't. She just did."

I waited yet again and would wait until everything had been said.

"She's been like this all damn morning. All whities in a wad about something."

"It's bullshit and isn't fair. Makes you just like everybody else, you know," Kyle said. "Say one thing and do another."

"We knew you couldn't be real."

Anna said, "I'm glad you're okay."

Kyle leered at her. "You can't forgive her just like that."

"I don't. But I am glad she's okay."

"So much for your stupid transparency and choice and challenge."

"I accept your anger and I deserve it," I said. "I violated your trust and our contract."

"You can't talk your way out of this."

"Kyle," Lydel said, "you're a whiney pussy. Ever since you got here. Whining about your elbow and gimping along on your broken leg. Now you're whining that the shrink let you down. You should be used to it. Everybody lets everyone down. She was gone. She's back. Accept it. It's not like she's going to cut you across the leg with a broken beer bottle."

"I'd rather have that."

"I bet you would."

"I never said a word about my elbow. Or leg."

"Is that what you were doing when you got here? Throwing yourself from the roof because you missed home?"

"Fuck that. I was fine."

Crack went Carmen's gum.

Kyle and I briefly looked at one another, waiting to see who would call off the bluff. We both knew she wasn't fine, that she'd had severe trouble adjusting, to the routines, to the constant chatter, to the next eighteen months of her life planned and sprawled in front of her. The first month she jumped from the roof, she started fights, spat at the staff, she refused to eat, took what few drugs she could get, and moved on and off the dismissal list, each time throwing herself futilely against the padded walls of the system, throwing herself most of all against herself.

"Nobody's fine when they get here."

"C'mon, Kyle, you tried to off yourself."

"Dying's fucking dumb. How stupid do you think I am? You're not going to die jumping from a one-story roof."

"Yeah, dying is fucking dumb, but guess what? You're gonna to have to do it someday."

"Until then, you're stuck with yourself, like it or not."

"Learn to like it. Learn to love it."

"I knew what I was doing. I always know what I'm doing—jumping, cutting, snorting—all of it. That's how I deal."

"By causing yourself more pain?" Anna asked, quietly.

"By *controlling* the kind of pain and when it happens. There's going to be pain anyway," Kyle said.

Unimpressed, looking toward the doorway, Lydel said, "Who the fuck are you?"

The girl in the threshold wore no lipstick or make-up of any kind. She dressed simply in jeans and a long sleeve shirt. She had the overwhelming, stark beauty of the not-quite-mature, and with it, the insinuation of loveliness to come. This girl would transform with her body. Her stride would lengthen with intent, focus. All the minute changes of all her preceding years would accrue into Aphrodite. The soul calls forth eros and metamorphosis.

Snap! went Lydel's gum.

"Nesha, please come in, sit down. Everyone this is Nesha. She'll be joining the group from now on."

"This is such bullshit," Kyle said. "You can't just bring a stranger in with no warning."

I could feel multiple stares on me and they were all correct. I hadn't thought through bringing a new participant into group, this group, especially without discussing it first. They all wanted one thing from me—the designation of value, for me to say, you, above all others, are valuable. You are important, loved, and destined for great things.

"You can't let her stay."

"It's okay Nesha. You can sit down. And you're right. I'm sorry. I should have discussed this before today, but I couldn't."

"You're just full of apologies."

The group went silent, dead.

Time dragged for another seventeen minutes until the alarm sounded. Relieved, the girls leapt for the door.

Snap! Went Carmen's gum.

Snap! Went Lydel's gum.

"Kyle?" Nesha said. "Kind of name is that? That's a boy's name."

Then the slap of skin on skin. Screaming. And the thuds of bodies hitting the floor.

Kyle had smacked Nesha. Lydel had tackled Kyle. They scuffled and wrestled as I reached under Lydel's arms and turned her to cuff her in a headlock. She slammed her fist into my jaw. We were on the lip of the small set of five stairs that led to the common area. I lost my footing, crashed and flopped down to the main floor. Kyle and Lydel soon followed in a tangle, with Kyle quickly regaining her position over Lydel to get in one last good slug before a CO pulled her off and another got a firm hold of Lydel.

"Get the fuck off me!" Kyle struggled futilely against the CO's hold.

Lydel crumpled forward, gasping, "I can't breathe."

"Take her to my office," I said, referring to Kyle.

"Against protocol."

"I don't care."

"Structure and consequences. We have to take her now."

"I don't fucking care! Get *her* to the infirmary and *her* to my office!"

Kyle and I sat across from one another. She was panting.

"Where the hell have you been?"

"One thing at a time," I said, avoiding the very thing and only thing to talk about. "Tell me why you hit Nesha."

"Screw that."

"Is that where we are? Still?" This was the wrong approach and I knew it. I was being too aggressive. "My proving and defending my role here and you angry and untrusting?"

"This your fucking fault."

"She picked on you about your name. You hear it all the time."

"Fuck you."

"You're angry."

"Yeah, and you also know that Nesha has jack-shit to do with it. Or Lydel."

"It wasn't *my* fist in Lydel's face, wasn't *my* knee that broke her ribs."

"She's a skinny bitch anyway."

I looked at her.

"Where the hell have you been? You look like shit."

She forced me to address the issue. Kyle had allowed herself to rely on me, need me. I saw her. I listened. And what had I done? Left. Just like everyone else. At the critical moment, I'd left. Just as she had begun to acknowledge that something important happens each week. Just as she had begun to look forward to seeing me, and through that, herself. Just as she had begun to recognize the relevance and specialness of our meetings and how, even after an hour of being there, she had the sense that no time had passed, no time at all.

"I'm sorry."

"You can't just do whatever the fuck you want. You can't make me trust you and then disappear!" She struggled not to cry.

"I'm on your side, Kyle. Just know that I'm always on your side." I held her gaze. I was sorry. I was helpless. "You know what this means?"

"Yeah, I know what it means."

"This is number three. This means you're gone. County." Everything's lost. Back into the system proper. Because of failure. My failure.

Kyle looked away. "Whatever. I don't give a fuck."

A CO interrupted and handed me a set of transfer papers.

"Where were you? Someone die?"

"I took a trip."

"What is that vague bullshit?"

"Alice left me," I said. "Sort of."

"Sort of?"

"I saw her with someone else."

We sat quietly. Kyle looking at me and me looking at everything except Kyle. As we sat there, I knew I had failed her. My truancy turned me into another absent figure in her life, only one more devastating because she'd come to trust me. I have no legitimate excuse. My mind turned feeble. Briefly. We're all subject to weakness. My resilience had worn down to nubs. I had to get away. I know my job is in jeopardy. But that's what happened, where I was. My explanation. Kyle and I continued to sit quietly with one another, and I mindlessly shuffled the papers for some minutes, stunned, nursing my elbow, my shoulder, my jaw. I'd be sore later, I knew. Not too long before that day, I'd gone for a run and caught my foot on the lip of a crack in the cement. I pitched forward onto my forearms and knees. My skin was broken, scraped, nothing more than a little road rash, but I hadn't gone down easily, and I was sore for days afterward. The older you get, the harder you fall. I shuffled the papers. That's why I'm here, with all of you, giving you more detail than you wanted, justifying, telling, retelling. I had to because Kyle looked at me, fully, seeing everything, clearly, and said, "Before you sign those, if you're gonna sign those, let me tell you this one last thing. Listen here..."

CPSIA information can be obtained
at www.ICGtesting.com
Printed in the USA
FSHW021915301119
64460FS